PLEASE DON'T
TELL HER
I'M IN JAIL

PLEASE DON'T TELL HER I'M IN JAIL

A Kiss Under The Earthquake Rubble

LUKE OKOLI

authorHOUSE®

AuthorHouse™
1663 Liberty Drive
Bloomington, IN 47403
www.authorhouse.com
Phone: 1-800-839-8640

This is a work of fiction. All of the characters, names, incidents, organizations, and dialogue in this novel are either the products of the author's imagination or are used fictitiously.

Published by AuthorHouse   09/11/2012

ISBN: 978-1-4772-6282-5 (sc)
ISBN: 978-1-4772-6283-2 (e)

Library of Congress Control Number: 2012915354

This book is printed on acid-free paper.

DEDICATION

This book is dedicated to my beloved wife, Amaka Okoli, and my child, Sochima Luke Okoli.

CONTENTS

CHAPTER 1

"And this is what is called *the law of diminishing returns*," Mr. Ugba concluded his lecture in economics and left the classroom. The students began to rush to the door to catch the school bus to the South Eastern Campus of the University of Nigeria, Enugu, where the next class would take place in thirty minutes.

Mr. Ugba was the economics teacher at the University. *Ugba* was not his actual name but an a.k.a. given to him by the students. His name was Gipson Iroha. Mr. Iroha used *ugba* (an Igbo delicacy) to make references whenever he discussed economics terms such as: the law of diminishing returns, inflation, demand and supply, opportunity cost, etc. He used ugba so often that the students could not help re-christening him *Ugba*. Some students did not even know that his name was not *Ugba*.

It is typical of students to label a teacher with a word or words the teacher uses very often in the classroom. For example, if a teacher uses: *"You know,"* students are likely to dub him or her *"You Know."* If the teacher uses: *"so,"* they will re-christen him or her *"So."*

The rush to the next class was tense because the lecturer had hinted that there was going to be a short quiz today. For this reason, everybody was hurrying to catch the school bus. Nkiru was not in a hurry. She had a car with which she shuttled around the school campuses. Before the bus got to the South Eastern campus, she was already there. She usually gave a ride to her friends, first-come-first-served. Only a few students who had wealthy parents had the luxury of owning a car to get around the school.

Leisurely, Nkiru walked her way to the parking lot chatting with some friends. There was no need to hurry because she would be there before anyone else. When she got to her car, one of the students called her attention to a flat tire.

"Jesus have mercy!" Nkiru exclaimed. "I can't believe this. Flat tire? Incredible! Why now? I don't want to miss the quiz. Oooh, no, no, no! Why today, this car?"

She went around the car inspecting it. The other three tires were in good shape. She gazed at the electricity and telephone lines that criss-crossed above trying to figure out what to do. One by one her friends, who had assembled to ride with her, disappeared to catch the school bus. Nobody was left to assist her. More students were still coming out of the building, but everybody was in a rush to get to South Eastern campus. Nobody had time to look at Nkiru and her problem.

CHAPTER 2

Benjamin and Maximus rushed out. "Hey Max! Come here," Benjamin shouted, "Nkiru is still around, let's ride with her."

"Great!" said Max grabbing the door handle while Benji rushed over to the other side.

"Hold it men," said Nkiru despondently. "I have a flat tire."

"Oh me-e-n, this is crazy," said Max as he opened the door and scampered out flagging the last bus frantically.

"Hey Max," shouted Benjamin, "come here, let's help Nkiru to change her tire."

"I wish I could," replied Max still running. His trousers were dropping. "I don't want to miss the quiz."

"Oh boy," Benji sighed. "Now, let's see. We have no time to waste."

He stooped and studied the bad tire.

"Don't worry girl," Benji told Nkiru as he opened the boot. "I'll help you. Where's your spare tire?"

"I don't have one," Nkiru replied.

"Hail Mary! No spare tire?"

"None."

"Then where do we go from here?"

"Don't worry about me Benji," said Nkiru grimly. "I can miss the quiz. The last bus is still loading. Run for it or you will miss it."

"Leave you with a flat tire?"

"Don't worry. The worst is I'll miss the quiz. I can't kill myself."

"Do you realize that the quiz is part of the semester exam?"

"I do, but what can I do?"

"I can't leave you here."

"Don't worry Benji," Nkiru insisted hopelessly, "I'll be fine. I'll wait until I get help. Go and take the quiz."

"I'd rather not. Let's see if we can work out something here."

Benji was frustrated but he had the compassion to assist Nkiru. He would certainly miss the quiz. The Sociology lecturer had hinted that the quiz was crucial to the final exams. While he was speaking with Nkiru, the last bus left.

As he was wondering what to do, a lecturer drove by. He rushed to meet him, but the man was gone.

Another lecturer drove up. "Hey Sir! Hey Sir!" Benji yelled.

Dr. Francis Okafor looked through the window and saw a student running towards him. He slowed down. "I'm in a hurry to pick up my children from school, what's your problem?"

"Sorry Sir," Benji said humbly, his hands crossed behind his back, "we have a flat tire here and we have an exam at the South Eastern campus. Do you have a spare tire that I can borrow to get over to South Eastern? I'll bring it back this evening."

"A spare tire?"

"Yes Sir."

Dr. Okafor scratched his bald head. "Nobody has made this kind of request from me. Suppose I meet the same problem on the way, what do I do?"

"Sir, you're right. It's a possibility, but I pray it won't happen."

The man hesitated. He got out of his 504. His car was the model Nkiru had, but newer. Nkiru's car had seen many years of rugged roads and potholes. He opened his boot and asked Benji to lift the tire. "Make sure you bring it back to me today."

"I will Sir," Benji replied and rolled the tire to Nkiru's car. Benji's concern and kindness impressed Nkiru in no small measure.

Soon he had the tire mounted and Nkiru was back on the wheels

Nkiru and Benji did not miss the quiz after all. When they arrived at the South Eastern campus, the Sociology lecturer was just pulling up in the parking lot. Nkiru and Benji rejoiced. They were on time.

CHAPTER 3

Since the flat-tire incident, Nkiru had developed a special likeness for Benji. His help exemplified how people should make sacrifices for others when they are in need.

To pay Benji back, Nkiru reserved the front seat of her car exclusively for him. Nobody should take the front seat unless when Benji was not around. The back seat was for everybody, still on first-come-first-served.

One day Benji was one minute late to Nkiru's car. Max had rushed to take the front seat, but Nkiru stopped him.

"Go to the back seat Max," Nkiru said.

"No, I want to sit here," Max replied.

"No, you can't."

"Why not?"

"I said no. Go to the back seat before all the spaces are taken."

Max was still arguing when Benji came. He gently excused him and hopped onto the front seat. This did not sit well with Max. The worst was that, while he was talking, all the spaces at the back were occupied. Nkiru had 8 passengers, five at the back, and three in front. No wonder the tire gave up.

They drove off. Max was left behind. He was really offended. "Why should she deny me the seat and give it to Benji?" he asked himself as Nkiru and her overloaded car raced down the hill. Max was infuriated. His situation worsened when he tried to catch the last bus but it was gone. For twenty-five minutes he was looking for the means to get to South Eastern. Later, he took an *okada* (motorcycle transportation). By the time he got to the South Eastern Campus, the lecture had gone half way.

A week later, Max confronted Nkiru at the cafeteria, "Tell me, why did you treat me the way you did last time? Why did you insult me?"

"Insult you, how?" Nkiru asked with an earnest face.

Max was a skinny young man with a wisp of mustache. He had eyes turned weird by marijuana. "I wanted to get into your car, but you pushed me out and offered the seat to another guy who was late to your car. Is that fair? Your policy has always been first-come-first-served."

"I believe you know why." Nkiru replied resolutely.

"No, I don't."

"Well, last time I had a flat tire, Benji was calling you to help him change my tire, you did not even turn. You kept running and . . ."

"I'm not the only person that left the scene. Other guys left as well."

"But Benji specifically called your name. He did not call others."

"Is that why you insulted me in public, because you have a car?"

"Listen Max, don't say that. I told you to go to the back seat and . . ."

"Because the front seat was reserved for the King, or the right guy?"

"I don't know about that, but I have to pay Benji back for his kindness. You saw that I was stranded; you knew that I needed help at that point; none of you stopped to assist me. Benji did. You have always ridden with us Max, but since that tire incident, I have decided to reserve the front seat for Benji permanently. Did that ruffle some feathers? Yes it did. But that's my decision."

"Nonsense! You have another reason for reserving a seat for him. You're only making up excuses. After all, last month when your car would not start, all of us pushed it, didn't we?"

"I know, but this incident is different. I was abandoned. If I were to retaliate, I wouldn't allow any of you to sit in my car any more. All of you are still privileged to ride with me. But Benji will always have the front seat because of his impressive gentlemanly behaviour. Besides, the car is mine. I can use it any way I want."

This aggravated Max. "Well, I have no money to buy a car, but I hope to own one some day, a better car for that matter, not this old junk of yours. I won't ride it again."

"Suit yourself."

Max would not allow the emotional dust of the flat-tire incident to settle. He was bent on causing trouble each time he saw Nkiru. He now took the matter to a whole new level.

"I wouldn't take that junk as a gift," he told Nkiru during another confrontation.

"Yes, it's a piece of junk," Nkiru had replied, "but it takes us to South Eastern everyday. You can go and buy a Mercedes car, why wait? Fool!"

"You must not insult me.

"Mr. Car Owner. Buy your textbooks first before buying a car. Stupid!"

This annoyed Max. He stared at Nkiru as if to jump on her and squeeze her neck. "You must not insult me. If you don't know who I am, ask people. If you don't take time, I'll deal with you."

"Get out of my face! Who are you?"

"What did you say?"

"I said who are you? You're too small for me."

"Did you say I am too small?"

"You don't even come close," Nkiru said with explicit pride.

"Is that what you say?"

"Quote me anywhere, you are too small."

"*Pull a hair from my palm.* I'm going to teach you a lesson."

"To hell with your threat."

"You will see."

"Nonsense!"

CHAPTER 4

The assistance Benji gave to Nkiru the day she had a flat tire had brought the two students closer. Nkiru had developed a great interest in Benji, and vise versa. They were seen often riding alone. One could safely say that they were in love. Nkiru loved Benji and was ready to go to any length with him. But she was afraid of one thing: her father.

Nkiru's father, Chief Igboanugo Aninwede of Akpugo-Ani village, was one of the richest men in Umueze town near Enugu. He was very successful in his contracting business. Chief Aninwede's growth hit its peak after the Nigerian-Biafra civil war. He was one of those contractors who made millions in the reconstruction industry after the Biafran war. At that time, the old brigade contractors like R.O. Nkwocha, F.F.B.C Nwankwo, Chief Osita Agwuna, C. T. Onyekwelu, Arthur One Thousand, and a host of others, were slowly phasing out of the contracting business in Eastern Nigeria.

Chief Aninwede had two wives and many children. He loved all his children but had special interest in Nkiru. Nkiru's mother attributed this to her daughter's dogged fight with an illness when she was only six years. Everybody thought Nkiru was going to die. She was only a skeleton. The illness twisted, warped, and wrinkled her skin so badly that it looked creased and craggy like that of a ninety-year-old woman. Miraculously, the little girl pulled through the terrible illness and was alive today.

From that time, Nkiru became her father's darling. She was considered fragile like an egg, and must be handled with care. Chief Aninwede gave orders that under no circumstances should anybody hurt his baby.

This was the genesis of Aninwede's love for Nkiru. On top of that, Nkiru was a bright star in the school. She was very intelligent and well-behaved. She topped the class from primary one to primary six, and from junior to senior secondary school. For this and other reasons, her father loved her so dearly.

Nkiru had grown to be a 21-year-old law student. Her classmates liked her because she was nice and kind to everybody. Sometimes she helped students with money.

One day, one of her classmates, Maggie Echeruo, stopped at her table in the cafeteria and asked if she would eat with her. Maggie had run out of her money and was starving. Nkiru not only allowed Maggie to eat, but also bought more food for both of them. Before they left the cafeteria, Nkiru gave Maggie some money. "Take this," she said, "it will *keep the wolves out of the door, until a better time comes round.* If you need anything, stop by my room."

Nkiru was openhearted and liberal. A benign young lady, she was very compassionate and easily drawn to tears when she saw someone in difficulty. She would sell her soul to help somebody. She was nice inwardly. Outwardly, she was pretty, black, slender, and tall like her mother.

CHAPTER 5

Max was seeking vengeance against Nkiru and Benji. He insisted on getting even for what he claimed Nkiru and Benji did to him. One day, on his way to the South Eastern Campus, he saw Benji on the school bus and said,

"Hey man, how come you're ridding the bus like us, the poor?"

"What do you mean?" Benji replied, his face tight.

"I mean you are supposed to ride in your friend's luxury car. What are you doing on the school bus?"

"Listen Max, respect yourself," Benji said and removed his sunshades. "I believe you're old enough to reason like an adult. However, if you prefer to behave irrationally, you should know the class of people to talk with, not me."

That response drew the attention of students on the bus. They began to laugh and jeer at Max. He was annoyed because the students were laughing and cracking jokes at his expense. Neither he nor Benji said anything further, but their hearts were apparently loaded with indignation.

The next day, Max saw Benji in the Library and went to him,

"Benji, I do not like the way you talked to me yesterday on the bus."

"Excuse me Max, I don't have time for any talk," Benji replied putting a pencil between the pages of his book. "This is exam time and everybody is busy working on his or her books. I do not want to be bothered with anything that does not relate to study."

"So you think I'm crazy talking to you, eh?"

"If you are saying something reasonable, definitely, I'll listen to you, but not when you are talking nonsense, why should I waste my precious time listening to you?"

"Benji, who is talking nonsense? Your insults have reached a peak. You know I can deal with you."

Benji did not respond. He bent down and continued reading. He could not concentrate because Max was still ranting and making threats.

"Do you realize I can deal with you fool?" Max said intimidatingly.

"The best way I would advise you to deal with me is to beat me in the exam. Even in natural strength, you know I am stronger. But I'm not interested in fighting. Men are more civilized today, except idiots like you. Today, people demonstrate what they can do by showing their talents and potentials."

"Do you write my papers for me during exams?" Max asked biting his lips.

"I don't, but you flunk every paper," Benji replied widening his eyes.

"And you are worried because you pay my school fees?"

"I don't pay your school fees, but it's a waste to whoever that pays it because you do nothing in school than loafing about."

Max was hurt. He looked steadily at Benji without saying a word, and then he said: "Benji, if you don't take time I'll ruin your life."

"You're too small to do that," Benji replied and packed his books. He was tired of this exchange of nothingness.

"Let's bet," Max said in anger extending his little finger to Benji. "I will deal with you."

"You cannot do anything. You can't face me. By the way, what are you doing here? I have never seen you in the library. Go to the gathering of the nincompoops and ruffians where you belong. This place is for the serious minds. Stupid wreck!"

With that, Benji left, leaving the simmering Max behind. The intense exchange had attracted many eyes that were looking at Max as if he had entered the women's restroom. They had never seen him in the library.

Outside the building a schoolmate saw Benji and asked him what was going on between him and Max.

"That boy is useless," said Benji adjusting his belt. "I don't know what the idiot thinks he is doing in school. He floats about like *a broken piece of gourd on a riverbank,* never bothered about his studies. He takes the last position after each test."

"Let me tell you something," said the schoolmate calmly. "That boy is dangerous, make no mistake about it. He is evil. He is as serious as a heart attack in his threats."

"I don't care what he is," said Benji boldly. "If he is a devil, he should go with the devils. He can't do me any harm."

"You'll not believe it," said the boy, "but I can tell you that Max is bad. He is in a cult."

"Well if he is in a cult, he should mingle with the cultists, not me. I'm not in a cult."

That piece of advice from the classmate was factual. It sank with Benji. He just discovered that Max was a cult member. He was a notorious member of a devilish gang in the school. He took part in the killing of a student in the Western Point University a year ago. He was expelled from that school. He was not jailed because there was no evidence linking him to the murder. He transferred to South Eastern University and formed another gang. Last year, his cult fought with another cult. Two students were brutally wounded. His cult once threatened to kill a teacher because he gave three students, including Max, an "F" after an exam.

Max was a devilish gang leader in the school. Throughout his school career, he was a non-performer. He began playing truancy from primary school. He had never passed any class but was promoted to a new class when he began to age out of the old class. A mischievous hooligan, he could never study his book. He was rough, violent, and dangerous. His parents tried to help him, but Max chose the evil way. Now he planned to attack Benji, and possibly Nkiru.

CHAPTER 6

South Eastern University had many dormitories. The female dorms were located at the Northern part of the school, while the boys' dormitories were located at the Southern part. At the boys' dorms, Benji shared a large room with four boys.

Max was determined to fulfill his vow to attack Benji and Nkiru. He had consulted with his cult members. He had secretly gathered information about the subjects' dormitory locations, room numbers, and itinerary. He gave his boys guns to shoot Benji and Nkiru in their dormitory rooms. The gang planned to execute the plot on a Saturday night when most students would be away partying and socializing. Max was aware that Benji did not attend parties or social clubs, and must be in the dormitory.

Benji was not unaware of the criminal activities of thugs and cults in many schools in the country. He knew that such fiendish groups existed in many Universities, and that one such group was in South Eastern University. He was also aware of the crime and killings they committed within and outside the school. But since he had nothing to do with them, he went about his business like every student. However, after some friends had warned him to watch his back, he became more careful about his movements.

Nkiru had earlier warned Benji to be ware of Max, "He is very dangerous," she told him. "He could harm you. Make sure you lock your door before you sleep."

"He can't do anything to me," Benji had boasted.

"I know you are physically stronger than he is," said Nkiru, a little worried, "but this is not a question of one-on-one physical combat. This is cult. They carry guns. They kill lecturers, they kill students, they kill their enemies, and they kill themselves too. They commit grisly murder without cause. Stories of the heinous crimes cult gangs commit in different schools are on newspaper headlines every day. You must listen to me. These boys are dangerous. I don't want anything to happen to you."

Benji loved Nkiru so much. He would never neglect her advice. Outwardly, he pretended he was not afraid of anybody, but inwardly, he paid attention to Nkiru's advice and henceforth, strove to avoid any further confrontation with Max.

One Saturday night, when many students were out as usual for amusements, Benji was in his room reading. His roommates were all gone. After a while, he began to have a hunch. He remembered Nkiru's advice and knitted his brow in deep thought. His gut feelings told him to leave the room. As he was going to the door, a voice from the window shouted: "Stop!"

Benji did not stop. He grabbed the door-knob instantly. He saw a figure climbing the window. Before he could get out, there was a loud bang from the window. He dashed out feeling some pains on his right thigh. He had been shot. He managed to drag himself into room number 50-E where some students were having a party.

The students heard the shot and panicked. They led Benji in, locked the door, stopped the music, switched off the lights, and remained quiet. They were afraid that the assailants might follow Benji to their room and begin to shoot everybody. They hid Benji under the bed. Everybody knew the viciousness of "Alpha Mayhem Fraternity" on the campus.

After about an hour, nothing happened. The students brought out Benji who was bleeding. They bandaged his wound and rushed him to the hospital. The shot missed his femur but tore through the ligaments and muscle tissues of his thigh. He was lucky that the gunman was not well positioned.

CHAPTER 7

"Didn't I tell you to beware of those hoodlums?" Nkiru reprimanded Benji at his hospital bed. "They kill people easily."

"Yea, you told me," Benji agreed with a groan. He was in pain.

"It's painful?"

"O yea. It's killing me."

"You will be alright, sweetie."

"I hope so."

Shortly after, nurse Chidimma arrived with her *vital signs* apparatus. Nkiru made a move to leave the room. "Oh no, you don't have to go," said the nurse. "Sit on the chair while I check his BP."

Nkiru was pleased. She didn't want to go.

"Nurse, may I ask you a question," said Nkiru, a little nervous, "how bad is the wound?"

"Oh, it's not bad at all. Three bullets were extracted from his leg; none of them touched the bone. He was lucky."

"Oh! thank God," Nkiru sighed as she tried to help the nurse tidy the other side of the bed.

"The wound is healing fine," continued nurse Chidimma, "I believe in a few days the doctor will discharge him."

"O thank God," Nkiru said.

Nkiru was appreciative of the humane and devoted manner this nurse was treating Benji. She fumbled in her purse and came up with something she clutched in her palm. When nurse Chidimma turned to leave, Nkiru rushed forward to pass some money to her.

"Oh no, you don't have to do that," the nurse said. "I'm doing my job."

"Take it," Nkiru insisted, "I'm impressed the way you are performing your job."

"I understand, and thank you for the compliment, but I'm doing what I'm supposed to do. It's my duty."

Two days later, Benji was discharged with a pair of crutches. He went to the village to continue his convalescence.

"You must change that school after this," Nkiru told him. "You will not go back to that damned school."

"I was nursing the same idea," Benji agreed. "I want to stay away from those devils. And you should change school too."

"I have applied already."

Nkiru was not in her dorm the night Benji was attacked. She was in the village.

CHAPTER 8

Two years had passed. Benji had graduated and was working at the Nigerian Electrical Power Authority (NEPA) Enugu. Nkiru graduated the following year and secured a job at the Addis & Lillian Law Firm Inc.

Nkiru had rented a three bedroom flat at Independence Layout Enugu with her best friend, Cheluchi Udenka.

Benji was squatting temporarily with a friend at Obiagu, a slum area in Enugu. He was looking for a one bedroom flat that he could afford. He had a lot of responsibilities at home. His younger siblings were in school, and he was responsible for their school fees. He also assisted his father financially. Therefore, he must economize his income. He could not afford a luxury life like young civil servants.

A two bedroom apartment came out within the housing complex where Nkiru lived. She quickly alerted Benji. "I'd prefer a one bedroom house," Benji told her.

"Get your stuff and move in here before someone takes it."

"I can't afford it me-e-n. It's expensive. I need just one bedroom."

Nkiru wanted Benji to live close by her, so she would keep an eye on him. She didn't want any woman to snatch him. There were a lot of desperate girls around.

Nkiru and Benji were in true love. They had become emotionally bonded together since the shooting incident at school. They pledged to remain together the rest of their lives. They had planned to get married after their graduation and Nkiru had been working towards this. She had told her friends that as soon as they got a few things out of the way, they would announce their wedding.

"Listen Benji, you can spend eternity looking for a one-bedroom flat. Many low income workers are looking for one bedroom, it is scarce. This is an opportunity for you to get a house. Take the two bedrooms."

"If I have the means," Benji replied, "I'd like two bedrooms, but I can't afford it now."

"I'll help you make the first payment," Nkiru told him.

"Really?"

"Yes. You have to move in before somebody takes the apartment."

CHAPTER 9

Nkiru could hardly pass a week without visiting home. She went home on the weekend and her father, Chief Igboanugo Aninwede, confronted her,

"I understand you still entertain the idea of marrying Anigbo's son against my wish?"

"Papa, I love that boy."

"At your age, love is an illusion, do you know that?"

"Papa, I thought we have settled this issue," Nkiru replied a little irritated. "Why don't you leave this matter alone?"

"I won't," said the Chief authoritatively. "You must not marry that destitute boy whose father is impoverished and has no social worth in this village. I told you that as soon as you were ready for marriage, I would find you a young man with high portfolio; a man from a respectable family; and a man with social recognition like your father. Definitely, not this brat."

"Suppose I don't like your choice?"

"I'll find another one."

"And if I don't like that one either?"

"I'll continue to search until I find your heart's desire," Chief Aninwede said persuasively. "And listen, I do not want to continue this dialogue with you. You must obey what I said. I'm sure you understand your father's status in this village and must channel your thoughts, desires, and lifestyle to fit into it."

"Papa, that age has gone-by. Do you think that a graduate like your daughter is not informed enough to know what is good for her? Do you consider me not bright and intelligent enough to know what I want? Papa, you are letting me down."

"You got it wrong. Many young women make mistakes because of love infatuation. Later, they will regret it. I believe your education has given you all the exposure and wisdom in the world to pilot your affairs successfully. You are smart too, I know it. But . . ."

"Then leave me to live my life," Nkiru interrupted angrily. "Leave me to make my choice of a man."

"Of course you can make your choice, provided your choice falls within my preference. It must fit into my status in this village, that's the main point. I cannot betroth you to a wretched beggar, whose father is unknown and without social significance. Never! You have all the liberty in the world to make your choice, but it must be someone with some distinction. Your choice must meet the requirements of Chief Igboanugo Aninwede of Akpugo-Ani, period!"

Nkiru was still speaking when the Chief turned and went away with the rhythm of a great man. That was his style.

CHAPTER 10

Nkiru skipped six weekend visits for three consecutive times because she didn't want to confront her father. She hated his irksome harassments over her decision to marry Benji Anigbo. Despite the man's objection, Nkiru had made up her mind to marry Benji. He was the only man she loved on earth and she had made this clear to her parents.

Her mother had no problem with Benji nor his family. Inwardly, she was predisposed in his favour by virtue of his affable personality. At the same time, she internalized her husband's position—that Nkiru must marry a man from a responsible family where she would be happy. The woman was somewhat on the fence, ready to set sail with whoever that won the day. But she knew that her daughter would lose because her husband would never give in. She wanted to stay out of it or else the Chief would descend on her.

Nkiru had told Benji about her encounter with her father in the village.

"So he is still having an antithetical view about our plan?" Benji had asked.

"He is more resolute in his stand than ever."

"Well, I can't help it," Benji said emphatically. "I'm sorry, I must marry you. It's you, or nobody. Did you make him understand my position?"

"Talking of your position? He hates to hear your name mentioned."

"There are many couples who got married without their parents' approval. I'll marry you, my baby, come rain, come sunshine."

"I'd rather marry with my parents' consent than not. My father has high status in the community. The action will dent his image."

Benji contoured his face. "What's that suppose to mean? What are you talking about sweetie?" He held Nkiru close to himself patting her hair. "Are you having a second thought?"

"God forbid!"

"Then why did you make that statement? Is his social persuasion more important than our life?"

"Hmmmm!" Nkiru sighed. "I'm caught in a web. *This is a case of a hooked spear rammed into the belly; pull it out, you draw the intestine; leave it inside, it poisons the system.*"

"To me, our future is more important," Benji declared and kissed Nkiru in the forehead. "We must think about us darling."

Nkiru coiled her hands around his neck solemnly, "I know my father more than you do. He is a terrible man. He is tough."

"What is he going to do, kill us?"

"That's not beyond his whims, I swear."

"Then we must elope."

"I'll find a way out," Nkiru said, almost in tears. She buried her head on Benji's shoulder in a true love, affection, and helplessness. "I'll find a way to bend his will."

Chapter 11

In the village, Chief Igboanugo Aninwede got information that, despite his objection, Benji had moved into his daughter's house. He flew into a rage.

"Enyidie, Enyidie!" the Chief called out to his wife.

"Yes, my husband."

"Did you hear the latest news about your daughter?"

"What is it?" the woman panicked. "Is she okay?"

"That stupid boy has moved into my daughter's house in Enugu. He can't even rent a house. That's the hooligan that will marry my daughter. Over my dead body."

"Who told you this?" replied his wife, her voice sounding conspiratorial. "Do you monitor your daughter's life from here?"

"Is that what you say?" the Chief asked bluntly. "I know who has been *fanning this ember*. You are supporting this child in what she is doing. I know it. Anyway, *when the rain falls, everybody will get drenched.* When I take the step I will take in this ignominious business, everybody will regret it."

"What have I done, my husband? Did I give your daughter to the Anigbos? Please, I haven't done anything. *See my armpit, it has no hairs.* Give your daughter to whomever you like. I don't want anybody to involve me in this. I never advised Nkiru to marry Anigbo's son."

"While I'm encouraging this girl to find a man of noble class; a wealthy man with social consideration; and a man worthy to be my son in-law; you are busy collaborating with her and aiding her disobedience. How many times have I warned you to stop entertaining that idiot when he comes here? Each time he comes here, you serve him with food like a prince. The next time I see him in my house, I will . . ."

"My husband," his wife protested, "Anigbo's son does not come here to look for me. He comes here to see your daughter. When did we start to discriminate against visitors—who should be served and who should not? I'll tell Nkiru to stop the young man from coming here, if that would bring peace."

"I'm not here to argue with you. I already know what I'll do."

Nkiru's mother was afraid. Her husband's threat must not be taken lightly.

CHAPTER 12

After that exchange, Chief Aninwede took his walking stick and left the house still boiling within. He arrived at Anigbo's house in the next village and met Benji's father cracking palm kernel and chewing roasted dried corn.

Anigbo wasn't that old, but years of penury and deprivation had cast shadows under his eyes. You could count his bones and the number of black hairs in his head. He looked more like one who had a marasmus disease. He wore an unbuttoned, stained shirt that was way too small for him. His knickers were also scruffy. These tattered clothes were Benji's discarded old school uniform.

"I have come to see you," said Chief Aninwede without greetings, his face tense.

"Ha ha ha! Akuilighili, welcome to my house." Anigbo greeted the Chief warmly in his title name. He felt honoured to be visited by such a dignitary. He was looking around for a stool to offer his august visitor. There was none.

"Don't worry about a seat," the Chief said with inflated ego. "I don't want to sit down. The reason why I'm here is to tell you to warn your son to take his hands off my daughter. If not, *between two things, one will happen.* Did you hear me well?"

Anigbo was taken aback. He stared at the chief in confusion holding the stone in one hand and the roasted corn in the other. "Aninwede calm down," he said nervously, "help me understand this. What is wrong?"

"Your son is after my daughter for whatever reason. There are many girls in this village to marry. Tell him to find another woman that suits his social status, not my daughter."

Anigbo now understood the problem. "Sit down, let me find you some collar?"

"Don't worry about collar," he said and turned to leave. "Did you hear what I said?"

"I have heard you," the man replied without malice. "I'll tell my son what you said. But I thought that those of you who know better advise us to exercise flexibility on some issues regarding our cultures and traditions."

"What are you talking about?" Chief Aninwede asked bluntly, looking down on Benji's father. "Did you say we advised you to abandon our culture?"

"No, I didn't say that. I said, we hear knowledgeable people like you telling us that civilization has eroded most of our way of life, and that we should take things as they come."

"Meaning?"

"Meaning that we should try to accommodate some changes in the way we live. For example, in the past, parents chose who their children would marry. Today, it's the opposite. Children hook up with their partners or spouses and inform their parents later. Some don't even tell their parents that they are getting married. This is in contrast to the tradition. So which way do we go?"

"Nonsense!" Chief Aninwede retorted provocatively. "That's not what I am here to discuss. I have told you what is in my mind. If that stupid boy does not leave my daughter alone, something will happen."

"Aninwede!" Anigbo shouted angrily, "your last statement was obnoxious. What will happen? What 'thing' will happen?"

Anigbo stood up with a poignant face showing his uneven teeth as he spoke. He never liked Aninwede, nor did anybody in the village. His hatred for the Chief was sharpened into a rage because of his threat to his son. *Not what was said, but how it was said, that ruffled the feather.* Flailing a finger at the visitor aggressively, Anigbo said,

"If anything happens to Benji my son, I will tell you whom you have met. I don't care about your wealth, I don't care who you are, if anything . . ."

"Look at this man," Chief Aninwede was rattled at Anigbo's audacious response. "Look, he has the courage to talk to me. Who are you talking to?"

"You! I'm talking to you. Who are you? *Do people go to their homes through your compound?* Do you feed me? I don't care about your money. If I see a tiny scratch on my boy, I'll show you that *hot water can kill the tortoise.*"

"Ha ha ha," Aninwede scorned. "Slut. You're playing with fire."

"You are about to cook with petrol," Anigbo returned, his eyes fierce.

The noise of their exchange flew across the neighbours' fences.

"I have to go because people will be wondering who Chief Aninwede is talking to. But I'm sure you got my message. The next time your son sets foot in my compound, you will hear the story."

"Leave my house before I break your head," Anigbo charged raising a stone

"House indeed! My dog would not live in your house."

CHAPTER 13

Chief Aninwede's visit to Anigbo's house tipped the balance of peace in the poor man's quiet life. He was deeply worried about Benji's safety. He was infuriated. He felt that the rich treated the poor badly. He blamed his creator for making him poor. If I were wealthy like that idiot, Anigbo spoke to himself, would he have the guts to talk to me the way he did? I don't blame him. I blame my god for making me wretched.

The next day, Anigbo went to the market to sell some yams. He met his neighbour, Ikejiani, a freckle-faced middle-aged farmer, who also came to sell some items, a fowl and a bunch of unripe plantain. "How are your kids?" Anigbo greeted Ikejiani.

"They are fine," Ikejiani responded as he spread some feed on the ground for his fowl to beef up its weight. The more a fowl weighs when it's picked up, the more money it attracted from buyers. "I heard some loud exchange in your house yesterday evening, and I said I would stop by to check if everything was okay. I've never heard a noise in your house since your wife's death."

"My brother," Anigbo replied, "it's this useless man they call Akuilighili (surplus wealth). He answers Akuilighili, yet no man has ever tasted his wealth."

"Is he the one that contested the local government chairmanship election and failed?"

"Exactly. He is mean."

"What brought him to your house in the first place?" Ikejiani asked as he offered his friend his snuff. "I know he doesn't go to poor people."

"Thank you my brother," said Anigbo, as he took the snuff. He cleaned his left palm on his knee, and tipped small measure of the black substance in his palm amidst the conversation and began to scoop the snuff into his nostril using his thumb-nail. "This man came to my house yesterday and warned me to tell my son to take his hands off his daughter. He spoke to me very disrespectfully with threats."

"That's his style," said Ikejiani, blowing his nose. "I know him very well. He has no regards for people like us."

"Not a bit. He didn't even greet me or respond to my greetings. He simply bumped in and began to talk. I tried to calm him down, offering him a seat. He wouldn't listen to me but continued to rattle. I was upset, but I managed to control my anger. However, when he said that 'if my son still meddles with his daughter, *between two things, one would happen,*' I got annoyed and asked him what would happen? I told him that if anything happened to my son, I would show him that, even though I was poor, I could teach him a bitter lesson."

"Does he want to criminalize you because your son is in love with his daughter?"

"The baboon should answer that question, not me," Anigbo replied.

"He is too arrogant and saucy."

"He is."

"Is his daughter pregnant?" Ikejiani asked.

"No."

"Well, *the matter has no legs,* said Ikejiani adjusting his cap, ready to leave. "If his daughter was pregnant by your son, that would be a different story."

"Even at that?"

"Which of your sons are we talking about?"

"My first son, Benji."

"Is Benji interested in his daughter?" Ikejiani asked and picked up his walking stick.

"Who knows? Children of today, mingle freely. I do see the young lady in my house at times."

"Well, if Aninwede does not want your son to marry his daughter, he should tell his daughter not to come to your house looking for your son."

"That's right. And if I come to his house with wine to make a proposal on behalf of my son, the fool should reject the wine."

"Right. He has no business warning you to stop your son from disturbing his daughter."

"He is stupid, otherwise he would know the right thing to do."

"I hate him. He is very mean and arrogant. There's nothing wrong in being proud, however, you don't allow your pride to overflow its bank into other people's crops."

"Thank you! Nobody likes him. Everybody holds him in total contempt."

"But you must be careful," Ikejiani spoke in a low voice. "Remember, he was associated with the murder of Owo's brother. He lost his credibility in the community after that incident, and critics are still mauling his name. He is not someone with a valid claim of eminence among the elders."

"I know. But he cannot touch my son," Anigbo said resolutely. "I don't care how many people he had killed.

I told him that if he touches a single hair of my son, I'd destroy him."

Home folks believe that people can use charms or *juju* to kill other people.

CHAPTER 14

A week later, Ikejiani was attending a clan meeting where he met Chief Igboanugo Aninwede. Chief Aninwede said to him,

"Look here *nwokem* (man), go and tell your friend, the one they call Anigbo, to . . .

"Aninwede don't you know my name any more?" Ikejiani interrupted. "Why do you have to address me that way? My name is not *Nwokem.*"

"What do you mean?"

"What do I mean? Is *nwokem* my name? Don't you know my name?"

"That's not an issue," he grinned sardonically.

"It's an issue. I'm an *ozo* title holder, and must be addressed as such. You should call me by my name, or you can address me by my title: *akalucha ngene?*" (The stone the builders rejected . . .)

"Sit down," Aninwede retorted pompously. "Who cares about those porous titles you people take on without merit? They are meaningless."

"To you it's meaningless, to me, my name and my title are important."

Ikejiani was irritated. Some members of the gathering had converged to see what was going on. Although he was not rich, Ikejiani, a short man with a dropping shoulder, was revered for his wisdom.

"You people assume portentous titles without meriting them," Aninwede declared. "That's empty clout. Well meaning people who take these titles don't just take them for taking sake. They merit them. They contribute to the affairs of the land. They give to the community, they help the poor."

"What have you done for the community?" Ikejiani challenged, still fuming. "Tell me, what have you done for our people since you became established?"

"I can't stand here talking with you," said the Chief contemptuously, "it's degrading for me. I can call you any name I want. Who are you, to start with?"

"Listen, Aninwede, or whatever they call you, *you've got a tiger by the tail without knowing. Fie aka nanya* (be careful). I'm not Anigbo. If you make the mistake of getting into my life, I'll tell you that men are strong but some men are stronger."

"That's empty words," the Chief replied insolently. "I can't think of anything you can do. Listen, ask questions, I've *swallowed what swallowed an elephant.* You are only a little bug that can be crushed with a toe?"

"Is that what you say?" Ikejiani said, his face crimson.

"Yes, that's what I said. You're nothing."

Ikejiani looked at him for a few moments and said, "I don't need to waste time with a talkative. *Dogs that bark much run when it's time to bite.* Fool!"

"Hold it, hold it my people," pleaded Nnaji Okoh, a member at the gathering. Okoh was trying to make peace between the two. "Chief Aninwede, I greet you. Mazi Ikejiani, I greet . . ."

"Who gave him *Mazi* title?" Chief Aninwede turned to Okoh. "Why should you append *Mazi title* to his name? Who is he?"

"I believe that all of us have self-respect," Okoh said. "No matter how poor we are. People have their self-esteem and self-worth. Therefore . . ."

"Nwokem, I don't want to hear that," Aninwede said. "By the way, who appointed you a mediator over this matter? Who are you? Did I ask you to make peace?"

"This is how he insults people," said Ikejiani. "Useless man."

"What did you say?" Chief Aninwede charged raising his walking stick.

"I said you are a useless man," Ikejiani repeated loudly and sprang to his feet. He was seething with anger. "You are a useless man. I said so. Talking to you was the biggest mistake of my life, fool!"

There was a noisy exchange between Chief Aninwede on one hand, Ikejiani and Nnaji, on the other. People were not happy because the commotion was disrupting the gathering. They were particularly distraught about Chief Aninwede's querulous behaviour. He could not be controlled. The chairman of the meeting had to appeal for calm. He advised members to respect one another and focus their attention on the social issues they had come to discuss. He made allusions to Chief Aninwede over his belligerent behaviour. Aninwede felt offended by the chairman's remarks. He picked up his walking stick and stormed out of the meeting cursing everybody.

CHAPTER 15

"Benji, what are you doing?" Cheluchi called from her house. "Would you come here a minute?

Benji was taking a nap. It was five o'clock in the evening. He put a shirt on and went down stairs. Cheluchi was in the living room drinking.

"I have some beer," she said. "Do you care to join me?"

"O, sure!" Benji replied and slumped onto the sofa. He picked up a glass.

Occasionally the three friends, Benji, Cheluchi, and Nkiru, bought some beer and enjoyed themselves, sometimes with other friends. Once in a while they went out to eat. Today, Nkiru was not home. She went to the village to see her parents.

At first, when Benji entered the room, he noticed that Cheluchi was a little over—casual in her dress. She had never dressed like that in his presence. Her top was virtually exposing her breasts. She wore no bra. When she bent forward to fill her glass, her breasts were in plain view, dangling seductively.

Benji pretended he did not see it. He stole a look or two every now and then. Sometimes Nkiru dressed casually too, particularly during the hot weather. But Cheluchi's appearance this evening seemed deliberate and dangerously inviting.

When they finished their drinks, Cheluchi excused herself and went into her bedroom. A minute later, she called Benji from inside, and asked him to come and assist her to arrange some heavy stuff. It wasn't unusual for the girls to ask Benji for assistance when they needed his help. Benji was always willing to help them to shift their beds, shift refrigerators or dressers, hang pictures on the wall, and things like that. He was available to help get their electronics working again. He did man-job stuff for the ladies just for asking.

Today, innocently, he went into Cheluchi's bedroom to assist her. When he walked in, Cheluchi briskly pushed him forward and locked the door. She put the key in her pocket so that nobody could get out. She had stripped off her petty blouse and greeted Benji with her exposed body. The sight of her naked body was both charming and magnetic. She smiled at Benji who was embarrassed.

"Girl, what are you up to?" Benji asked with a wry grin. He was confused. His eyes were fixed on Cheluchi's pretty-looking bare chest. It was irresistible. Her breasts were exposed and enticing, extremely youngish pair. No man can resist grabbing them.

Cheluchi was pretty, as pretty as Nkiru. She was slim and fair. The sight of her naked body—soft, luscious, and succulent—spewed a wave of nervous twitch in Benji's system.

It was difficult to understand why Cheluchi was doing this. She was Nkiru's best friend and was to be her chief bridesmaid during her up-coming wedding. Nkiru would not believe it if a fortuneteller or some mystic powers told her that such a thing could happen behind her back. She and Cheluchi were very close. Was Cheluchi drunk? Was she attacked by a spate of libidinal surge? What on earth could've provoked this bizarre behaviour? Or does she want to snatch Benji from Nkiru, her best friend?

Benji shrugged his shoulders at the sight of Cheluchi's charming figure. He knew what the girl wanted. Boys always know. It's rare for a woman to experience a breakdown of the superego checks and balances. Benji struggled with two alternatives—grab this wholesome thing and dive into the bed, or tuck his thing behind his back and retreat? Which way? He didn't know what to do.

"Do you want it?" Cheluchi asked him again and again moving closer to him.

"Want what?" he asked, as if he did not understand.

"All for you Ben," said Cheluchi pressing her chest on Benji's body. "What are you waiting for?"

As her breast caressed his body, a thrilling wave of erotic sensation electrified his nerves.

"Hmmmm!" Benji moaned. "Eemmm, emmm, I . . ."

"Come on, be a man. I shouldn't have to do all this coaxing. You should know better. Don't pretend."

"Listen, you are my fiancé's best friend, I . . . I can't . . ."

"Who cares? How much does it matter? Variety is the spice of life. You have not experienced me and vice versa. I want it now, right now! We shall cement it. Have fun baby."

This wasn't the first time Cheluchi had attempted this foul game. On several occasions, she had tried to lure Benji to bed, but he resisted. Today, she was more determined. Nkiru was not home, so why couldn't they enjoy themselves. Nobody would know. Nobody would find out. And nobody would tell. Besides, it's not a numerical mass that can be quantified, nor does it leave a trace after a visit. So, why not?

Cheluchi applied every feminine tactic in her arsenal to compel her best friend's man to go to bed with her. Benji was a principled man who always had his wits about him. In as much as he liked Cheluchi and her gorgeous attributes, he did not want to offend Nkiru. He loved Nkiru so dearly and never wanted to do anything that would hurt her feelings. He was a devoted lover. Nkiru knew this, and she trusted him one hundred percent. She also had confidence in her friend, Cheluchi. They liked each other and did things together. Their friendship started many years ago when they were young secondary school girls. But human beings can change.

"Cheluchi," Benji said, trying to calm the sexually charged girl, "you don't want me to do this to your best friend."

She pulled him by the hand going to bed, "Nobody will tell her, come with me."

"Women have no secrets," said Benji philosophically refusing to follow her. "Nkiru will hear this some day if it happens."

"I disagree. Women may discuss what they did with their husbands at night, but not what they did with a man outside marriage."

"Really?"

"Only a fool will reveal what she did in private with another man. Come on, behave. I need it right now."

"You're drunk baby."

"Perhaps, but I need you, handsome. The door is locked, what are you waiting for?"

Benji gaped at the young girl lustfully. Cheluchi had a wonderful body structure with shapely legs. She had tantalizing hips. Her naked body radiated splendour. She had the most alluring feminine outline with the most thrilling body configuration on earth. Her nudity could disarm any gunman. The sight of her naked body was breath-taking. Benji was almost trembling.

"I can't do it," Benji told her earnestly. "I must not do this. Don't be offended, but this is . . ."

"Stupid!" Cheluchi shouted, getting weary of begging. "This is strictly between you and me. She won't know. Who will tell her?"

"News flies."

"This one has no wings."

She folded her arms around Benji's neck. "Carry me to the bed, I want to feel your . . ."

"No. Stop! I can't do it. I have great respect for my fiancé and I have respect for you too. Besides, I have my dignity to protect. There is no way I can go to bed with you. If you were not Nkiru's best friend, that's a different story, and I . . . I . . ."

"Nonsense!" Cheluchi snapped. "You are a fool. *How can you spit out honey dropped in your mouth?* Get out! Get out of my room."

She opened the door, pushed Benji out, and slammed the door.

Jesus deliver me! Cheluchi screamed in her heart after shutting the door.

Mabel was sitting in the parlour. No one knew she was there. When Cheluchi opened the door, Mabel shot a suspicious glance at her. She was certain that Mabel saw her naked body. Benji was equally shocked to see Mabel sitting in the parlour. They did not know that somebody was there.

Trouble! Mabel might have heard them too. How could Benji deny this? How on earth could anyone believe that he didn't do anything?

Good Lord, save Thy child! Benji prayed in his heart as he chatted with Mabel. This is crazy. Someone has observed this nasty scenario.

Inside her room, Cheluchi sat on her bed recounting what had happened. Nkiru is going to hear this, she said to herself, Mabel will tell her. She will say she saw me naked with Benji. Ooooooh! I'm finished. What a temptation! The worst is that Mabel might have heard all I was saying to Benji.

At the parlour, Benji was sitting beside Mabel and talking with her. Her looks explained her thought. Mabel was suspicious of what was going on between these two people, but she did not say anything. Is this what they do when Nkiru is away? she speculated. Oh, this is obnoxious. What a mess! Nkiru does not know the type of man she is soon to wed, neither does she know the type of girl friend she has. Poor her.

"Where is Nkiru?" Mabel asked Benji, trying to conceal the loaded thoughts in her mind.

"She went to the village," Benji replied, still battling with the thoughts of what had just taken place. He knew that Mabel saw Cheluchi stark naked at the door. He was certain that Mabel was going to reveal all she saw.

At the time Benji and Cheluchi were in the bedroom, they did not know that the entrance door to the palour was not in lock. Most of the time, that door was never locked. Their friends and neighbours could walk in just like that. Mabel was one of Nkiru's group of friends who lived in the neighborhood and who dropped in occasionally. Often she came over to see them. Nkiru's group of friends liked her so much and frequently converged in her house to chat, to watch games, or to socialize.

Cheluchi was ashamed so she did not come out of the room. She remained inside while Benji and Mabel conversed. She was certain that Nkiru would be greeted with this bad news as soon as she stepped in. Mabel would tell her everything, no doubt.

CHAPTER 16

Benji did not sleep that night. He woke up in the morning in a bruised spirit over what happened the previous day. He was totally devastated even though he was innocent. However, he was satisfied that he did not yield to Cheluchi's sexual storm. He congratulated himself for resisting her crazy amorous madness. But he did not know what Cheluchi was scheming.

On Sunday evening, Nkiru came back from the village. Immediately she stepped in the house, Cheluchi led her into the bedroom, "I have bad news for you," she said panting. Her intention was to preempt Mabel.

"What is it?" Nkiru panicked. "What happened? Everybody okay? Is Benji all right?"

"Sit down." Cheluchi said.

Nkiru sat at the edge of the bed. Her heart began to beat faster. Her eyes were on Cheluchi's lips.

"On Saturday afternoon," Cheluchi began, "Benji knocked on the door. I opened the door. He came in and took me by the hand and led me into my bedroom and began to romance, kiss and fondle me. I . . ."

"What!" Nkiru shouted and stood up. "What!"

"I told him to stop, but he would not. He overpowered me, pushed me into the bed and raped me."

"Oooh my God! Ooooooh!" Nkiru began to weep.

"I was under him crying and begging him to release me. I was asking him how he could do this to me. He did not listen until he had satisfied himself. And then he knelt down and begged me not to tell you. He had tried this animalistic act before unsuccessfully, I was afraid to tell you."

"Benji did what?" Nkiru asked in tears. "I can hardly believe this."

"Ask him. I have a witness."

"Did you say Benji did this?" Nkiru continued to ask in disbelief, her lips dry and trembling.

"When this was going on, he did not know that Mabel came in and was sitting in the parlour. Mabel probably heard me crying and struggling to free myself. Ask her, she saw me naked when I pushed Benji out of my room."

"Ooooh, my world is shattered," Nkiru wept bitterly. She collapsed on the floor.

After recovering from the shock, Nkiru sprang to her feet and raced upstairs. She began to bang at Benji's door. Benji had no problem discerning who was hitting his door in this manner. Someone must have told her what happened, he thought.

He opened the door. "Baam!" Nkiru slapped him. A spark of fire flashed in his eyes. "What were you doing with Chelcie in my absence?" she ranted. She called Cheluchi Chelcie. "What were you doing with her, *mkpi* (he-goat or bitch)?"

"Sit down NK (short for Nkiru), let me expla . . ."

Baam! Nkiru slapped again with the right hand.

"O no, let me . . ."

Baam! she slapped with the left hand.

"Bitch! I have a bitch for a husband. I did not realize you were a first-class whore. No doubt, this is what you do each time I am not around. You were only caught today. You went as far as forcing her. It's over! Go your way, I've gone my way. I thought you loved me. It's over! The wedding is cancelled."

Benji was hurt in the eye. The second slap hit the right eye hard. After that, she banged the door and left.

Nkiru did not give Benji a chance to respond. But Benji hoped to explain everything when she calmed down. He took Nkiru's reaction with a great equanimity. For Benji, the problem still remained who would believe his explanation. With all the glaring evidence, who on earth would believe he didn't do it? It is well known that men lie when they cheat. So Nkiru could hardly be convinced to the contrary. Cheluchi presented her story in such a succinct way that Nkiru had no reason to doubt her. Besides, there was an eye-witness account. This lent credibility to her fabricated tale.

Benji sat in his room totally confused. His eye had swollen. Cheluchi, obviously, told Nkiru the story upside-down, he thought. This is a typical case of *injuring a person and winning the adjudication therein.* The world is full of deceptive people, Benji said to himself in distress. How can I explain this to Nkiru to make her understand exactly what happened?

He lay flat in his bed trying to piece things together. He decided to give Nkiru time to cool down after which he would go and give her the true version of the story. My conscience is clear, he consoled himself. I'm innocent.

He looked in the mirror; his right eye was swollen and Nkiru's fingers were printed on his temple. He swallowed the humiliation.

CHAPTER 17

The following day after work, Benji came downstairs to Nkiru's apartment and knocked at the door. Nkiru opened the door. Seeing it was Benji, she slammed the door with force, almost heating his face. Benji pleaded from outside, begging her to listen to his own version of the story. "I'm on my knees darling; allow me to tell you what actually happened. I didn't do it."

"Bitch." Nkiru replied from within. "I have nothing to do with you anymore. I loved you with all my heart; I gave my life to you; and this is what I get. Go your way, I've gone my way forever."

"I didn't do it."

"Lie."

"You're mine."

"God forbid!"

"Yes, you are."

"Not Nkiru."

"You're my world."

"No more, we're through."

"I'm innocent of this accusation."

"Bitch! Mabel confirmed it."

"You have not heard my part of the story."

"My ears are already bursting with what I have heard so far. I don't want to hear any more mess."

"I know I'm still yours," Benji continued to claim.

"No, you're not."

"Would you please listen to me for a minute, for God's sake?"

"Never! You betrayed me. Shame on you, bitch."

"You love me, I know this."

"Before."

"You still love me, my angel."

"Tufia kwa! *(God forbid)* Who is your angel? Hypocrite.

"I care for you, my love."

"You care for them. I have often watched how you look at her while we eat. You've been longing for it."

"I didn't do it."

"Shut up! There's ample evidence."

"I love you with all my heart."

"Beast! I don't want to see your face any more. The more I see you, the more your evil deed pierces my heart. Go to her, rapist."

Benji remained on his knees outside the door pleading and begging for an audience, but Nkiru and her friend, Cheluchi, were inside laughing and chattering.

He got tired and left.

One week passed and nothing happened. There was no change in Nkiru's position. Benji tried again and again to explain what transpired in her absence, but Nkiru had decided not to talk to him or have anything to do with him any more. At one point, Benji got irritated and decided to forget her, at least for now, and to allow time to heal her wound. *There's no point trying to take oxygen from a burning house,* Benji advised himself.

The love Benji had for Nkiru would not let him make a final decision to forget her forever. He put himself in her shoes. She did not understand, he told himself. If she were to grasp the true story of what happened, she would behave differently.

CHAPTER 18

Two months later, Lambert Nzekwe, Benji's friend, told Benji about an opportunity to travel to the United States of America for further studies. Benji was excited. He liked the news. He had been dreaming about this. This was an opportunity young men in Nigeria were praying for. He and Lambert began to plan to take a chance.

Traveling to America for further studies, especially for young people, is a rigorous undertaking. It was difficult to get a visa.

Since they had no money or sponsor, Lambert and Benji decided to do what boys were doing—go to Gambia, Ivory Coast, or Sierra Leon and apply for a traveling visa. It was much easier in those countries.

The two friends had been working on this project for months without anybody knowing. They did not want anybody to know because people might ruin their plans.

If they were in good terms, Benji would've revealed the plan to Nkiru. He had always shared his private matters with her. But as things stood, he decided to keep his business to himself. She will hear it when I'm gone, he told himself. This was also a good opportunity for me to get away from this charged environment.

Before he left Nigeria, Benji reflected on what took place between him and Cheluchi. He congratulated himself for refusing to yield to the girl's pressure; for resisting what he described as the breath-taking nudity of her charming image. He remembered, in particular, when Cheluchi drew closer to him rubbing her sensational nipples on his body, and at the same time, trying to unbutton his shorts. That was the most tempting moment. The Angels might have clapped hands for Benji for resisting the irresistible fresh kill. Only a few men could muster such a gargantuan of self-restraint. He did this because of the woman he loved, Nkiru. Most men would nibble a mouthful and run. Benji did not.

Three weeks later, Nkiru heard that Benji had left the country. Lambert's girl friend had visited and told her that Lambert and Benji were in Koutonou, enroute to the United States of America. Nkiru began to cry. She wondered if she had acted too harshly on Benji. She regretted that she did not have any discussion with him before he left. She felt she had towed too hard a line in the matter. She blamed herself for not allowing Benji to say something in his defense. I think I was ruthless with the whole thing, she thought.

In the weeks that followed, Nkiru did not sleep. She mourned Benji's departure as though he was dead. She recalled their pleasant moments; intimate discussions, loving moments, and future plans. A flawless relationship had existed between us, she thought, until the day the tide of his testosterone overflowed its pouch. I should've forgiven him because most men are like that. Oh! Benji my soul. Will he ever talk to me again? I think I overreacted.

CHAPTER 19

In August 2006, Benji, Lambert, and three other young men from Nigeria, arrived in Haiti on their second leg to the USA. They were promised everything, ranging from housing to employment, from scholarships to cars, and so on. They were delighted and full of hopes. The man who led them in the journey to Haiti was Tajji Coleman, a notorious drug agent from Mexico. The travelers did not know who Tajji was, nor his true identity, neither did they know the secret of the trip. He told them that he was recruiting them for a manufacturing company overseas. Tajji was specialized in recruiting drug runners for drug cartels in Southern America and beyond.

Tajji ran this recruitment trip for the *Bizooma* drug syndicate, one of the narco-traffic organizations operating at the Amazon basin in Southern and Central America. Countries like Honduras, Guatemala, El-Salvador, Jamaica, Ecuador, and Mexico, were some of the areas the drug cartels operated. Tajji shuttled to different parts of the African and Asian continents to recruit young men for the drug-smuggling business. The job of the recruits was to convey drugs to various parts of Southern America, Mexico, and the United States. Initially, the boys had no idea of the kind of work Tajji promised them until one morning when they were assembled for a briefing by the Drug kingpin, Captain Jeremiah Hudu.

Captain Hudu was from Ecuador. He was a middle-aged man, short and stout. His eyes moved with terrifying connectivity. He had an innocent face but the heart of a lion. Captain Hudu, popularly called, *Capt. Jerry,* was a mercenary soldier who fought in the Nicaragua civil war. After the war, he drifted aimlessly for a while around the Caribbean countries and later found treasure in the drug business. He was one of the most dangerous drug lords that operated in that region. For years, Capt. Jerry eluded captivity by the anti-drug squads and government security agents that hunted drug dealers in those areas. He and his lieutenants controlled over three hundred men who worked for them in the Amazon rain forest. In his address, Capt. Jerry said,

"Gentlemen congratulations!" He spoke with a Hispanic accent. "You've been employed to work for this organization. Your duty is to transport some "items" across the rivers and the creeks in the cover of darkness. You'll be under the protection of our gunmen throughout the trip. Once you have completed the first trip, you'll get used to it. Your salary is fabulous, very attractive. We pay handsomely. Those who work diligently, devotedly, and advance the course of this organization, receive rapid promotions and astonishing allowances. You can easily become a millionaire if you work hard. The sky is your limit."

At the mention of 'millionaire,' Lambert and Benji looked at each other.

"Therefore, it's up to you to put in your best. However, anybody who tries to be smart or tries to play some little game to the detriment of this syndicate, will have himself to blame. In a few days, you will be going to Naputu Creek for your first assignment. You will always have armed escorts who have tremendous knowledge of this vast woodland. Sometimes you will pass through swampy creeks in the dead of night; sometimes through a thick jungle; sometimes through the rocky mountains, etc. It's a challenging task, but anyone who endures to the end, will reap the fruit of his labour."

The address was laced with motivation and promises. It was inspirational to the adventurers. It gave some candidates a spark; to some, bolstered spirits. To some candidates, it was a disappointment and fear. Lambert and Benji went to a corner to analyze the briefing.

Clasping his hands behind his head Lambert said, "*Dianyi,* (My friend) I never knew this was what we would fall in for."

"Lord have mercy," Benji snapped tartly. His face was grim and despondent. The revelation had sent his temperature sky high. He looked at Lambert reproachfully, "Is this a dream? Why didn't you investigate before accepting this mess?"

"I didn't know," replied Lambert defensively, "My friend, Bamidele, painted the picture in a specious way that sounded amazing. He told me that we would be working in the banana and sugar-cane plantations, and that we could easily migrate to the US from there. He too might not have known what we were getting, until now."

"Gosh! Jesus come," Benji sighed, his face arid. "We are doomed. There are bumpy roads ahead."

"No doubt," Lambert agreed. "This might be the style the syndicate uses to lure people into their illegal business."

Benji could not hide his frustration. They knew it was too late to go back to Nigeria, nor is it safe to bolt? Besides, anybody who attempted to escape would be shot on sight. During trips, the escorts stayed in front, in the middle, and behind the convoy. So it would be suicidal to make any sneaky move. Moreover, unless you were escorted in or out of the rain forest, you could not know where you were heading to. There were many drug tracks that weaved in and out of the thick jungle familiar only to the veteran escorts.

"What do you think?" Lambert asked Benji. He was ambivalent.

"It's difficult to think of a new plan. We have no alternative. We will take it."

"I believe you," Lambert said hastily. "Let's give it a shot. All we want is money."

"It was never my ambition to do this dirty business."

"Me either," Lambert said. "But we've been roped in by this crime syndicate."

"Yes we have. We have to do it. After one or two trips we plan escape."

"I agree with you," said Lambert in absolute good faith. "That's exactly what I am thinking. After a trip or so we can flee. They say the United States is not far from here."

"Don't tell the guys from Nigeria about this plan," Benji advised. "I don't trust anybody, especially those Yoruba guys—Lanlokun and . . ."

"I am aware of that. It's just between you and me." The Yorubas are not reliable they are very treacherous."

"That's a sweeping statement," Benji pointed out.

"What do you mean?"

"Not all Yorubas are perfidious. Some are reliable, consistent, and unswerving. You seem to generalize."

"Benji, let me tell you," Lambert contended and rose from a dead branch where he sat, "have you forgotten what happened just before the Nigerian Biafra war? Chief Obafemi Awolowo and General Odumegwu Ojukwu reached a secret accord that if the Eastern Nigeria seceded from Nigeria, Awolowo will follow suit and declare "Omo Oduduwa" state for the Western Nigeria. What happened? When the East pulled away from Nigeria to become the Republic of Biafra, the Yoruba leaders, led by Chief Awolowo, not only changed their minds, but joined the North to wage war against Biafrans."

"That's a true story," Benji agreed, and slapped his leg to kill a moth.

"That's why I said that these people are not trustworthy. If you make any deal with any Yoruba man, don't rely completely on the individual because when the going gets tough, when the unexpected surfaces, or when there is danger, he will not only back away, but will betray you by divulging all the secrets he knows. Even the Yorubas don't dispute this. If you must make a deal with a Yoruba man, stand on your wits."

"Yes, we have to be careful how we communicate with our friends from Nigeria. These drug lords could be ruthless. If they hear any rumour about an escape plot, they can blow our heads off."

"Absolutely."

CHAPTER 20

First Trip. One evening, the drug runners were assembled, ready for the first trip. A camouflaged uniform was passed to each of them. A winter coat was also given to each person. After they had dressed up, they filed into a single chain to receive their one hundred and twenty pounds of cocaine pack, each.

Soon they were in the jungle heading towards the Kitengo waterway that led to one of the major archipelagos in the North of Haiti. It was a cold murky night. The sky was drilled with billions of stars. The crickets were shrieking in high pitched tones. The frogs, hibernating in the swampy marshland, sang incoherent choruses. Nocturnal creatures sprinted across pathways as the drug trekkers strode past. After about five miles of travel, a torrential rain broke out, falling in sheets. Benji was thoroughly soaked. He began to shiver. He said all the prayers in the world for survival.

After six weeks of travel to different places, the drug dealers returned to the base in Haiti. The first trip was hitch-free. No encounter with border platoons or security agents. So were the second and third trips. The boys were rich overnight. Their salary was handsome, US dollars. During the off days, they went to town, and enjoyed themselves. They banked their money and did other things. Most boys from Africa and Asia had the tendency to stash their money in the banks.

Benji and his friend, Lambert, seemed to have settled for the drug trafficking business. Since money started rolling in, they never thought about dusting up their escape plan.

"Dianyi, there's cash in this business," said Lambert one afternoon during an off day.

"Tell me about it," Benji replied counting his latest pay-packet—$1,500.00 for two weeks. "This is the easiest way to make money, me-e-n."

"It looks like we can hang on for sometime. What do you think?" Lambert asked.

"We will have one leg here, the other on the way out. But it's risky.

"I agree," Lambert noted slicing a large avocado fruit. "The problem is that the more you make money, the more you are tempted to push further on."

"I know. It's really tempting."

"Rex told me yesterday that a lot of boys die in this business," said Lambert.

"That River's State boy?" Benji asked.

"Yes. He has been here for a while. He has seen many ups and downs. This is the deal Ben," Lambert lowered his tone, "we have been here for a year, right?"

"Almost."

"Okay, let's give it one more year, if nothing happens to us, we call it quits and flee to US. What do you think?"

"That's not a bad idea. It all depends on our luck."

"Don't be afraid, we will survive," said Lambert confidently.

"I hope so, by God's grace."

CHAPTER 21

One year had passed since Benji left Nigeria, Nkiru was still mourning his departure. She would not forgive herself for not saying even goodbye to him before he travelled. She blamed herself for being heartless.

Until the truth was revealed, Nkiru believed she had good reason to treat Benji the way she did. It was an unwholesome act for him to rape my best friend, she told herself in one of her deliberations. How can he stoop so low? It was disgraceful. But . . . O Ben, she lamented. Where is he now, and what is he doing? Does he still care about me? He may have met someone else. Whores are all over America. But Ben is not that type. I know him. He is very selective and reserved. That's why I was heart-broken when he did what he did with Chelcie. If

I had talked with him before his departure, I would've told him to keep his love for me. I can't see myself living without Benji. Oooh no! I will die.

No day passed without Nkiru thinking about Benjamin. She became obsessed with the thought of Benji's wellbeing. She ate very little and subsequently began to lose weight. Her friend, Cheluchi noticed the change and knew why. Her conscience had been whipping her relentlessly since the day she piled up false accusation against innocent Benji. Each time she lay in her bed, she wondered what Benji would be thinking about her regarding the incident, and about her lies that had torn apart his relationship with Nkiru. She could not forgive herself for the crime she committed. I caused these two hearts to bleed, she often told herself. How can I explain this? What a liar I am! How can I make amends? Since the incident, I'm not settled at heart. How can I turn things around? Will they ever forgive me if I confessed? No! I'm not going to confess anything.

After three weeks, Cheluchi began to have some strange feeling of anxiety in her heart. When the pressure became so much, she went to the Church on a Saturday and had a confession. The exercise did not assuage nor lift her burden. The more she thought about the incident, the more she felt restless and heartbroken. Peace of mind eluded her.

While her friend, Nkiru, lay on her bed reeling in pains over the issue, Cheluchi was in her own bed lamenting over the fire she ignited; the fire that caused two hearts to burn. Would it solve any problem if I confessed my evil deed to Nkiru? she asked herself. I don't have peace of mind. I'm sure Nkiru does not. Oh, my best friend. And I'm sure Benji will never forgive me for the rest of his life. I am wicked. I am evil. Oh God, forgive me. Weighing all these things in her heart, Cheluchi broke down and wept.

Unable to cope with the pangs of remorse, Cheluchi made up her mind to reveal the secret to her friend. I can't be living like this, she said to herself, I must tell Nkiru the truth. She can kill me if she wants, I deserve it. I'm a whore of the first class. I don't know why I did what I did. May be I was drunk, but that's no excuse. Is it? she asked herself.

CHAPTER 22

A month later, after going through an unspeakable episode of depression, Cheluchi summoned courage and went to Nkiru. She met her lying in bed face up, as usual, moping at the ceiling.

"Nkiru," Cheluchi said, "I have something to tell you." She spoke softly like a fallen Nun or a repentant murderer.

Nkiru sat up, startled, and looked at Cheluchi with searching eyes. "Something to tell me?"

"Yes, a disclosure."

Nkiru's brow knitted in confusion. She pulled her legs out of bed sitting at the bedside. She signaled Cheluchi to sit by her side. "What are you disclosing?"

Cheluchi kept standing. "Promise me you won't kill me."

"What are you talking about Chelcie? What do you mean 'kill you'?"

Cheluchi did not reply. Nkiru was worried. "Did you hear anything about Benji?"

"No."

"Did you hear any news about my people in the village?"

"No."

"Did anybody die?"

"No."

"Then what are you disclosing? Come here honey. Sit down. What is it?"

Cheluchi began to cry. She sobbed profusely. Nkiru was puzzled. She tried to pacify her, at the same time she was afraid and eager to hear what she had to say.

Nkiru took a towel and dried Chelcie's face, "Now tell me what is on your mind, I don't care what it is. *No matter what the eye sees, it can't shed blood but tears.* Tell me."

"It's something you wouldn't like to hear."

"Jesus is Lord!" Nkiru panicked, "Benji is dead?"

"Not that."

She heaved a sigh of temporary relief. "Then what? Tell me."

"It's about the sin I committed against you."

"Against me?"

"Yes."

Nkiru stared in a different direction for a moment trying to think. "Hmmm! This is strange. What sin, what is it?"

"I lied to you, and I must disclose it to you. You can kill me or disown me, if you want. I deserve to die. I'm not worthy to be your friend. The devil played on my head and I became crazy and acted stupidly, irresponsibly, and grossly dishonestly. Consequently I caused you a very painful . . ."

"Get to the point," said Nkiru impatiently, "this merry-go-round is enough. What happened, what did you do?"

Nkiru was getting more impatient.

"Will you forgive me?" Cheluchi pleaded.

"Yes. There's nothing I cannot forgive you. You are my best friend. We have been friends since childhood. You are a sister to me. I'll forgive you for anything, but get to the point."

Nkiru's mind never came close to what package her friend had for her. Her imagination raced from one minor offense to the other, things like breaking an expensive dish; burning a costly dress with hot iron; or gossiping behind one's back.

Cheluchi was sitting at the edge of the bed now. Nkiru had pulled her to her side affectionately. She looked blank, but inside, she was loaded with stuff. "Oh! What a world of evil!" she said and looked at Nkiru ruefully.

"Say it," Nkiru urged her. "You are my best friend, I can forgive you anything. Say it."

"I lied. I lied to you about Benji. He never raped me. I made up the story."

"Eh!" Nkiru jumped up from the bed and stared at the guilty face. "Cheluchi! What did you say now?"

Cheluchi could not talk.

"What did I hear you say?"

"Forgive me, please? I deserve your wrath."

"Continue. How did it happen, bitch?"

"I was drunk . . . and . . . and I called Benji into my room pretending that I needed his help to lift some heavy stuff. He came in and I locked the door behind us and . . . I . . . wanted . . . him to . . ."

"Ehe! To do what?" Nkiru barked like a wounded lion, her face tense and horrifying. Cheluchi had never seen her face turn so fierce-looking. "You wanted him to do what, bitch?"

"I'm sorry," Cheluchi began to cry again.

Baam! Nkiru slapped her mouth. "Shut up!"

"Please . . ."

Baam! Another slap in the eye. She followed it up with a kick that sent Cheluchi crashing into the television stand. "Eve! Sorry indeed. Did he do it, animal?"

"No," Cheluchi replied covering her face in shame, "he refused. He never touched me. I tried to persuade him, but Ben . . ."

"Stop! *Ashawo"* (whore), Nkiru roared delivering another slap in her mouth. "Don't ever call him Ben any more," "His name is Benjamin. No more Ben."

"Benjamin would not succumb."

"And you were naked?"

"Yes."

"Really? So my boy was innocent. Oh! Poor Ben. And I kept vilifying and castigating him." Nkiru began to cry. "Oh Cheluchi, you have killed me. So you have the heart to do this to me, your best friend. You did this to me."

"It's the devil," Cheluchi wept. "I deserve death."

"Oh, who else can be trusted? So if Ben had accepted your offer, you guys would've . . . Ooooooh!"

"I'm evil, kill me," Cheluchi pleaded hopelessly.

"What a bizarre behaviour!"

"It's temptation. It was the devil."

"Get the devil out of this," Nkiru fired. "It's your lust. I hate you."

"I don't blame you."

"I now believe that you actually slept with Chiamaka's husband. I had thought you were innocent of that accusation, and I put my life on the line trying to prove your innocence. I never knew you were a street harlot.

What the hell is your chemistry made of? What is it that makes you beg men for it? What a whore!"

"A whore is better than me. I'm worthless. I'm not worthy to be your friend."

Saying this Cheluchi sprang to her feet, ran into the kitchen, and came out with a knife and offered it to Nkiru, "Here, stab me NK, I deserve it. I deserve to die. I'm not worthy to live. Satan is better than I am. I want to die."

Nkiru ignored her drama. "If you want to commit suicide, that's your business. Oh life! What a difficult world! Who can be trusted? You, of all people. I'll never forget this. Is this a true story?"

"It is. I lied against an innocent man. Kill me, you're justified."

"Why did you lie to me?" Nkiru demanded full of rage.

"Because I feared that Benjamin would tell you exactly what happened and you would kill me."

"Lord have mercy. Life is a mess. Best friends are the ones you can rely on. How many true friends are there in the world?"

"Kill me NK, don't delay any further. Take this knife."

"Chelcie, why did you do this to me?" Nkiru began to sob. "Why? Why? Why?

She burst out and wept bitterly.

CHAPTER 23

Benji and his friend were making progress in Haiti. They had saved a good amount of money in their accounts at the Manor Bank in Puerto-au-Prince. It was exactly two years, August 2008, the time they projected for escape. Their strategy was to disappear in the jungle through a smuggling route to the Dominican Republic. From there, they would relocate to Peru, and then move to Mexico, from where they would sneak into the USA through the border. Each of them had saved enough money, not only to find their way to US, but also to start life there.

On second thought, they restructured their plan; instead of taking their flight in August, they shifted it to December when there would be a longer period of holidays. Also, the activities of the border guards were less egregious at Christmas time. That would be the ideal time to sneak across the border to the Dominican Republic. Both officials of the drug syndicate and their staff would vacate the drug production laboratory during Christmas time and scatter into different cities. In January, everybody would re-assemble at the depot to continue the illegal drug business.

Luck was in favour of Benji and Lambert. For the past two years, business was smooth and running. There had not been any serious attack by the government troopers or border rangers who burst in occasionally to dislodge the drug dealers from their locations in the interior of the rain forest. Long serving employees of this syndicate had seen many raids. For Benji and Lambert, life in the jungle seemed great and agreeable. They had money.

One fine day in December, things changed. The convoy of smugglers had just left the camp for the last trip before Christmas. As they were trudging along in the jungle heading towards the Elliot Creek, a helicopter hovered in the sky. The leader of the drug convoy ordered a halt. Everybody stopped and took cover.

After about an hour, the helicopter left. The convoy continued their journey. Such air surveillance was not unusual. The government forces patrolled the ground and the air checking drug traffickers.

A few hours later, the helicopter reappeared. At this time, the smugglers were in a flat, patched, grassland—a stretch of open plain field bereft of thickets. Three helicopters were in the sky this time flying very low. Before the leader of the convoy could give orders to take cover, the helicopters started shooting. The men panicked and began to scramble for cover. The grassland offered little hiding place.

Almost immediately, there was sporadic shooting from different directions in the forest. Unknown to the convoy, the security troopers were in ambush on the ground. Gun shots were raining from the air and from the ground. It was a gruesome mayhem. Men were screaming and diving for cover. Benji and Lambert ducked under a brush. Many drug carriers were killed, many wounded. Lambert was one of the wounded. Two bullets pierced his right side.

As Benji was trying to help Lambert move to a safer place, the ground troopers closed in and surrounded them. "Hands up!" they shouted. Corpses littered all over the place. Their loads of cocaine scattered everywhere. The government forces were many and with automatic weapons. The escorts of the drug convoy were armed, but were easily overpowered by the troopers. The security agents flushed out the rest of the drug traffickers from their hiding places. Only a few escaped out of forty men. This operation was one of the most successful raids by the rangers.

The surviving captives were ordered to dig a shallow grave where their dead colleagues were dumped. Lambert had lost a lot of blood, and when Benji checked to see how he was, he had bled to death. In tears and in a nervous wreck, Benji hauled him into the mass grave. That was a big blow to him.

The captured men were handcuffed and led to the outskirts of the jungle, where the police trucks were waiting. They were huddled into the vehicles and transported to the capital, Puerto-ou-Prince.

A few months later, Benji was serving a sixty-five-year sentence for drug trafficking. He was lucky to be alive. Some countries execute drug traffickers if they are caught. Others sentence them to life jail without parole. Perhaps some day, after serving his term, Benji will be a free man and return to Nigeria. By then, he would be 88 years old.

CHAPTER 24

In the first two months of Benji's incarceration, tears were the order of the day. His eyes were swollen and never dry. After some time, his tear pouch dried up. In prison, who cares about tears? Benji learned this fact very quickly. He had no alternative than to settle for existence in prison. Thus, prison became a permanent home around which he now organized his life.

Six Months into his sentence, Benji was gradually adapting to the prison life, but not without great endurance. The hard-labour in the prison was severe. He was getting used to starvation; to not seeing the face of the sun; to lack of communication with the rest of the world; to having a tiny room to sleep, for toilet, and for recreation. He was also getting used to the punishment by the waders; and above all, to the mischievous treatment of his fellow prisoners.

He hated the world. He hated his life. He thought about Lambert whom he lost in the Amazon jungle; about Nkiru whom he might not see again; about his father and his siblings, and even his mother who had died years ago. He thought about all his relatives, and his friends, and wondered if he would ever set foot again in his beloved country, Nigeria.

Life takes its true meaning in proportion to one's daily battles against suffering. The illegal business has not only punctured my career, but has ruined my entire world," Benji lamented sorrowfully. "So I'll remain here wasting away forever? So this is my portion in life. Oh, Heavens!"

The prison rules were rigid and diabolical. Everybody must abide by the orders. Benji was an obedient man. He had no problem with the penal regulations. He also held tenaciously to his religious faith. He prayed every morning. He went to the prison Chapel every Sunday for Mass. Father Anthony Woodley visited the prison to celebrate the Mass for the inmates. On the days that Father Woodley's Mass-servant did not show up, Benji assisted with Mass-serving. He used to be a Mass servant when he was a small boy.

Due to his excellent conduct in jail, some prison guards became interested in Benji. They chatted with him every once in a while. This relieved Benji's boredom. They found him to be a nice and intelligent young man, not a hardened criminal. They found that he was one of those convicts whose ambition in life careered into something they would not have, under normal circumstances, settle for. Prison warders can distinguish hardened, unrepentant, criminals from those who hit confinement by a sheer stroke of misfortune or through the dictates of their fate.

One day, one of the guards, Sergeant Chuck Parkman, told Benji, in the course of their conversation, that he had a friend from Africa whose name was: "Ife . . . Ife-n-yi . . ."

"Ifeanyi?" Benji helped.

"Yes, Ifeanyi. I can't pronounce it."

"That name is from my tribe," cried Benji. "That's my people's name. He must be from the South-Eastern part of Nigeria, the very place I came from."

"O really?"

"Yes. And we speak the same dialect."

"That's interesting," said Sgt. Parkman. "Then would you like him to visit you?"

"No!" replied Benji quickly. I don't want any home folks here. My people don't even know where I am. Don't ever tell anybody about me."

"No problem."

CHAPTER 25

Another day, Sgt. Parkman told Benji, during a conversation, that Ifeanyi was traveling to Nigeria. Benji remembered Nkiru and thought about sending her a message through the Nigerian man. Thoughts about Nkiru forced Benji to accept a visit by this man. Mr. Parkman brought Ifeanyi to the cell. From his prison cage, Benji looked out through the iron protector and spoke to the man:

> **Please tell Nkiru, my sweet-heart**
> **That my world has fallen apart**
> **Tell her that my condition is frail**
> **But don't tell her that I'm in jail**

You can tell her that I'm very sick
Tell her my mission turned bleak
Tell her I may not see her again
But don't tell her I'm in jail

Please tell Nkiru, my sweet-heart
That I love her with all my heart
Tell her not to wait for me again
But don't tell her I'm in jail

Tell her she can find someone new
Please don't tell her all you knew
Just say that my mission failed
But don't tell her I was jailed

Tell Nkiru, the love of my life,
That I'm here wasting my life,
Say that my adventure was in vain
But don't tell her I'm in jail

Things won't be the same again
She can find someone to retain
Someone that will never fail
But don't tell Nkiru I'm in jail

Tell her to cry less about my plight
Tell her to pray for me day and night

Tell her my hope has been nailed
But don't tell my baby I'm jailed

O Lord, life is bitter and tough.
O Lord, life is sour and rough
O Lord, I'm weak and frail
Don't tell her I'm in jail.

The message was delivered to Nkiru. Nothing was added and nothing was removed. As expected, Nkiru was devastated to learn that Benji was not doing well. It would be worse if she knew he was in jail. But that fact was concealed from her. Her heart was broken. She passed sleepless nights for days and weeks. There was no information in the message that would enable her to contact Benji. The messenger declined to answer any question nor reveal his own identity. He simply dropped the message to Nkiru and vanished like a messenger from heaven.

Not knowing what to do to establish contact with her fiancée, Nkiru began to plan a trip to the USA. I must find Ben wherever he is, she told herself as she lay restless. I will go to the United States and look for him. He must be in great distress. Oh, Ben! Oh my love. Are you alive? Hang onto life, I'll be there in a minute.

Nkiru began to prepare for the journey to US. She told her father that she was interested in pursuing her Masters degree. This was an ambition the Chief cherished.

It is prestigious in the society to send one's child overseas to study. Chief Aninwede did not waste time to make funds available to his daughter to pursue her career anywhere she wanted. He was pleased with this development because Benji would no longer be seeing his daughter.

CHAPTER 26

Benji had spent twelve months in prison. Life in prison was, to say the least, excruciating, especially when you have a long jail term to serve. In his cell, he saw life from a nihilist's perspective. Life became entirely a dreary and worthless abstract. Like the philosophers, every day he sat quietly in his small corner wondering the rationale of life. He couldn't help asking himself over and over why man was created and deposited on earth; for what purpose? A man is born today; he grows to an adult; he struggles for survival; and then he is old and dies; so what? What does it boil down to? What did he get? What's the point? What's the rationale? What's the underlying principle of life? Who can tell me? Hmmmmm!

Those were the contents of Benji's meditations while he pined away in prison.

For drug traffickers in Haitian penitentiaries, there was no parole. Benji must complete the 65-year jail. He had fallen into an ineluctable confinement for the better part of his life. By the time he would regain his freedom, his life would've been spent.

Having come to terms with life in prison, Benji believed that there was nothing more precious than freedom. That was the first thing he learned in prison—that prison was not a place for habitation; it might be for rehabilitation.

CHAPTER 27

On January 13, 2010, at about 5: p.m., tragedy struck in Haiti. A massive earthquake measuring 7.0 on the Richter Scale, wreaked havoc in the impoverished Caribbean country, killing at least 222,000 people and rendered many people homeless. The earthquake, which took place about 15 kilometres southwest of the capital, Port-au-Prince, was the most powerful earthquake to hit Haiti in a century. The rupture caused many buildings to collapse, including the Presidential Palace, the National Assembly Building, the Port-au-Prince Cathedral, the main Haitian prison, and dozens of houses and structures in Port-au-Prince, Jacmel, and other settlements in the region. Reports said that the catastrophic earthquake was felt in Cuba, more than 200 miles away. Among the countries in the Western Hemisphere, Haiti had had its fair share of earthquakes and other geological mishaps.

The prison infrastructure, where Benji was serving his jail term, was affected. Many of the structures were destroyed. As the prison buildings and structures crumbled, so did the rules and regulations of the prison. The ecological disaster caused the security walls around the penitentiary to give way. Many inmates died in the disaster. Those who survived, helped themselves to freedom. Benji was one of the survivors. Out of the cell, the prisoners dusted themselves up and melted into the society.

Benji Anigbo had nowhere to go. He did not know anybody or any place in Haiti. But he was smart. There were many relief organizations, medical teams, and rescue workers, helping the earthquake victims. He acted quickly and offered himself to the Red Cross for a volunteer service. Concealing his identity, Benji told Mr. Brandon Gardener, one of the top officials of the humanitarian organization, that he was a visitor from Africa on vacation. He offered to help in the rescue operation going on in Port-ou-Prince. Mr. Gardner needed many hands, so Benji, who spoke fluent English and French, to the man's delight, was recruited right away to assist the wounded.

Newsmen and women from all over the world poured into the devastated Caribbean nation in search of news about the earthquake. Aware of his situation, Benji avoided cameras. He did not want to be seen in the newspapers because someone might recognize him as an escaped prisoner. He kept away from the crowd. He adopted very low profile and kept himself busy working with Mr. Gardner. The man liked Benji so much. He confessed that he had never seen such a devoted, dedicated, and hardworking young man.

Benji worked tirelessly. He never rested until he was forced to take a break. It was now the fourth day of the earthquake. Hopes of recovering surviving victims had dwindled. By now, trapped victims that could not be reached were dying under the rubble. Cries for help were no more heard. But on the evening of the fourth day, rescuers picked up a faint voice of a trapped victim beneath the rubble calling for help. The voice could be heard clearly when you pressed your ear to a tiny crack on the fallen wall.

There were not enough excavating caterpillars to go round the areas where service was needed. Rescue workers at this site were digging with shovels and diggers. Hard slabs and twisted rods made progress very slow. Soon they succeeded in creating a small opening, only large enough to pass a raccoon through. A minute later, there was an aftershock. The ground shook vehemently causing rescue workers to run for life. The digging was suspended. Later, the rescue team resumed work. No one wanted to enter through the small opening to rescue the voice that was crying for help. Everybody was afraid that the cracked walls might cave in if there were to be another aftershock.

The voice of the victim was still coming from below. It continued to agitate the minds of the workers. Still nobody wanted to risk his or her life to squeeze through the tiny hole. The iron bars would not let the workers widen the opening. Benji volunteered to creep in. He was slim.

"Are you sure you want to do this?" Mr. Gardner asked him.

"Yes Sir," replied Benji, "I want to try."

He rolled up his trousers, made the sign of the cross, and put his head into the hole. It was dark. He couldn't see anything, but the voice was still coming. He squeezed his body into the hole like a snake. At last his shoes disappeared underground. Half of the room where he found himself was covered with slabs and debris. He did not see anybody. The voice was coming from the left flank of the heap. With the small touch-light in his kit, Benji began to search through the wreckage. Soon he discovered that the faint voice was coming from an adjacent room.

There was a connecting door to that room. Benji tried the door. It was locked. He was lying on his belly for lack of room to stand up. He managed to come to a sitting position. He found a heavy piece of rock and began to slam on the door. After a great effort, the door was broken. Still, he could not go in because a huge wall was resting on the door. "Gosh!" Benji sighed.

He could hear the voice fairly well now. It was a woman's voice, probably a young woman. Benji began to push the door. The wall was heavy. It was moving a little. If more hands were available, it would be better. He kept working on it until he was able to squeeze himself through the small opening. He was tired. He had been working for hours.

On moving further into the room, he stepped on something covered with fragments and debris. He suspected it was a dead body. He pointed his touch-light. He was right.

"Where are you?" Benji called.

"I'm here," the voice replied in English.

He kept working his way towards the victim. Cement blocks, rods, and heaps of debris formed a barrier reducing his efforts to reach this person. For hours he kept struggling, and at last, Benji found the victim. She was a young woman.

"Oooh, thank God," the girl cried in tears, her voice very faint. I'm safe at last."

"O yes," Benji replied, "but we are not out of the wood yet. It's going to be a long way out. Are you okay?"

"My leg is painful Sir," the girl said. "The right leg."

Her leg was pinned under a huge slab. Benji could not pull her out. Her body was covered with dust and wreckage. He began to clear the bricks and pieces of blocks in which the girl was buried. She was about seventeen years old, Benji estimated.

What is your name?" Benji asked holding her hand.

"Hattie," she replied.

"Haiti?"

"No, Hattie."

"Oh, Hattie."

CHAPTER 28

Above the ground, the rescue workers were waiting. They had lost communication with Benji, but they still heard faint voices deep down. They knew that he had found the trapped person. They were waiting for his instructions to determine how to proceed about lifting the victim. There were many barriers—twisted rods, mangled iron bars, huge concrete slabs, and corrugated iron sheets—everywhere.

From the way Benji was handling this earthquake victim, one would think he was a nurse. He learned many things from his First Aid training. As he was clearing the debris, there was a massive aftershock that shook the ground violently. Benji dived on top of Hattie, to protect her from being crushed by the falling walls. A sheet of wall landed on his back. Fortunately, the wall was partly wedged by an iron rail. A direct hit would've meant death for both of them.

The aftershock made matters worse. It sealed up the opening through which Benji was going to pull the victim to the surface. Now they were both trapped. There was little hope of getting out alive. If the workers above did not reach them in the next few hours, they would die. This was the fear many rescue workers entertained. That's why nobody wanted to risk going into the tunnel to save the trapped victim. Benji ventured and became a victim too.

"What happened?" Hattie panicked.

"I believe it's an aftershock," Benji replied.

"What is an aftershock?"

"An aftershock is a minor earth tremour or earthquake that usually follows the occurrence of a major earthquake. Sometimes it is as devastating as the earthquake itself."

Until now, Benji had never experienced an earthquake. However, he had read about earthquakes, erosions, volcanoes, hurricanes, windstorm, landslides, earth-tremours, cyclones, flood, and other natural disasters that take place in many parts of the world.

Earthquake is one of nature's most destructive forces. Africa is blessed, for compared to other continents of the world, African continent does not suffer a lot of geological and ecological disasters.

Above the ground, the activities of the rescue team had ceased. Benji and Hattie knew it was nighttime. Everywhere was quiet. When there was no activity, they knew it was night. When they began to hear voices and activities, they knew daytime had come. Twenty feet deep in the wreckage was as dark as hell.

At this point, Benji had been trapped for two days without food. Hattie had been there for almost six days, and her energy was receding rapidly. She had become highly dehydrated. Benji was feeling very weak also, yet he had been there for only two days.

"Keep hope alive, Hattie," Benji consoled her. "We will make it."

"Are you sure? The last earthquake or aftershock has sealed my hope of getting out alive."

"It shouldn't," Benji replied. "I'm confident we will survive."

"Oh God, what have I done?" Hattie began to cry.

She had cried a dozen times since Benji joined her in the underground ditch. She was in pain. Her leg was still stuck beneath a huge piece of slab. Right now she lacked the energy to cry or talk. She was extremely weak and desiccated.

"Oh, Blessed Virgin Mary, help me," she prayed.

"We will make it. Keep your spirit afloat, don't give up. The rescuers are working hard to reach us. Very soon they will excavate the rubble and deliver us."

"I'm so weak. I'm not sure I'll survive this ordeal. Can I ask you one thing?"

"What is that?" Benji asked curiously.

"Will you do it for me?"

"Yes."

"Are you sure?"

"What is it?"

"Kiss me before I die."

Benji was at loss. "What are you talking about?" he asked Hattie.

"You have taken all the pains to get here to save my life, and now your efforts are useless because I'm dying. I an hardly breath. I'm too weak. I know I won't be going out alive with you."

"You will not die. Hang on, we will get out soon."

"I know how I feel. I cannot survive this. Kiss me before I die.

"I'll kiss you, but you must not die."

She was yet speaking when Benji bent over and gave her a passionate kiss. He was now emotional.

She sighed and began to cry. "I can't breath."

"Hang on baby, they are coming to get us. Hang on."

"Oh, I'm dying. When I die, I'll be your Angel in heaven. You'll always have my love with you. Forever my love will shine down on you, guiding, and protecting you wherever you go."

"Stop saying all this," Benji was terrified. "You must not die. We'll survive, and I'll be with you."

CHAPTER 29

Hattie was going down steadily. Benji was worried. He began to wonder if she was going to make it. She rarely spoke now, and when she did, it was inaudible.

"I'm here for you," Benji said. "Keep up hope."

"I love you," she whispered to Benji. "If we survive, you will be mine, I'll be with you, and I'll be yours forever," Benji could hardly hear her faint voice.

"Let's survive first, summon your coping mechanism, I promise, you will be mine."

"I love you."

"I love you too," Benji replied and lifted her head. She could not hold her head up. It was hanging. A tear dropped from his eye "Lord, don't let this happen to me."

Above the ground, the excavating work continued. Mr. Gardner was worried about Benji's safety. He wondered what was going to happen to the young man he sent underground. In fear, he sent an urgent request to the officials to come immediately with a giant machine.

Time was not on the victims' side. Instead of sprinting like a cheetah, time crawled like a snail; so it seemed to the trapped victims. On the sixth day, work resumed. A huge concrete wall, which came down during the aftershock, was the target. All efforts were focused on removing this massive slab. Mr. Gardner was directing the operation. He believed that if the wall was removed, it would open the door to reaching the victims.

Successfully, the wall was dragged away. The rescue workers moved in with shovels and diggers.

Soon they heard a voice, "We're here. We're here. Keep coming to the left, to the left. Keep coming."

There was jubilation by the workers. The people beneath the ground were still alive. At last they saw Benji, twenty feet beneath the ground. He was covered with dust and filth. They moved in to pull him out but he told them to get the girl first.

"A huge block is pinning her down," said Benji. "We must carefully work on lifting it."

Benji was not sure whether Hattie was still breathing. The team began to work on raising the slab off her leg. They tied an iron cord on the slab and hooked it to the caterpillar. The machine pulled and pulled. Hattie's leg was free, but it was in bad shape.

When they emerged from the pit, Hattie was not breathing. "Oh! after all this," Benji began to cry. "Oh, my dear Hattie, come back. Don't do this to me."

The Red Cross team began to administer first aid on her. Suddenly, they felt her pulse. Hattie was revived. There was ovation among the rescue party. They carefully wrapped her up and rushed her to the hospital.

Hattie's parents and her three brothers were killed in the building. This was strictly kept away from her for the meantime.

CHAPTER 30

After three days of recuperating, Benji felt strong enough to move around. He had taken two days off. He went to the hospital to see Hattie. She was sleeping. The doctor said she was doing okay and that she would make it. Benji stood at her bedside watching the girl. She is pretty, he assessed. She is such a beautiful image. He could not help admiring the sleeping beauty.

Benji was right. Hattie was pretty. She was tall and slender. Her features were flawless. She had beautiful romantic eyes. The local people in Haiti called her *the beautiful one.* Before the earthquake, Hattie was preparing for a Miss Haiti Beauty Contest.

I must learn more about this girl, Benji told himself as he watched her. She is fascinating. Her beauty is captivating. In the rubble, I didn't realize she was this charming. This is my woman, he said as he headed back home.

What about Nkiru? he asked himself inwardly.

Nkiru may have discovered that I was in prison for life, he replied to his thought. Besides, I told her not to wait for me, but to find someone else. So it's likely she has married another man.

After two days, Benji went back to the hospital to see Hattie. He wanted to formally introduce himself to the girl, for she had not really seen him. While in the rubble, she only heard his voice, and she knew it was a man's voice. This time, Hattie was awake.

"Hattie," said Benji softly. "I'm the person who was in the rubble with you."

"Oooh my God," cried the girl. "Oooh my dear." She stretched out her arms for a hug.

Benji came closer and hugged her.

She was recovering but still unable to sit up. "I'm glad to see you. Thank you for saving my life."

"It's my pleasure," Benji replied, smiling. "I'm glad we made it out."

"You are a hero," she said studying Benji.

"You are the hero for holding onto life." Benji replied.

She beckoned Benji to come closer, "Don't forget what I told you in the rubble. We've survived the ordeal, and I'll be with you the rest of my life."

"I won't forget," Benji responded with a smile. He bent over and kissed her. "I promise, I will be with you. You will be mine forever."

That kiss fired a deep affection in Hattie. It caused a torrent wave of love to flow in her heart; a passionate love for the man who saved her life. She began to cry after that kiss. She held Benji's hand and would not let go.

"Please do not forget," she repeated.

"I promise."

Benji did not forget. Hattie had told him while they were trapped beneath the collapsed building, that she wanted to be with him forever. Benji had promised it would happen if they survived. He understood what Hattie meant by *don't forget*. Women don't often say: *I want you to marry me*? They would rather say, *I want to be with you;* or *I want you to be mine*; or *I want to be yours, take me*. Benji Anigbo was willing to take Hattie. He loved the young woman and had developed a great affection for her even in the rubble. He made up his mind he was going to marry her.

Hattie had fallen in love with Benji mostly for his self-transcendence—a vital instinctual value rarely found

117

in mortals. For when nobody was willing to venture into the wrecked building to rescue her, Benji volunteered. On his part, Benji was in love too. Seeing her in pain in the hospital bed touched the remotest part of his emotional fibers. It heightened his feelings of affection for Hattie. He vowed in his heart that he must marry her. He pledged that the protection he offered her in the rubble must continue forever. He was happy that he canceled his contract with Nkiru when he was in prison. Besides, Nkiru had told him that their relationship was over.

They talked for a while and then Benji left. Hattie forgot to ask Benji his name. All this while, she never knew Benji's name. What a fool! She blamed herself. When next he comes, I will ask his name. I'll also tell him that I love him so much, and that my love belongs to him as long as I live; that I'll love him till water dries up in the ocean; that I'll never forget the way he kissed me in the rubble; and that I'm dreaming of the day when he'll belong to me forever. She hoped to reveal details of her heart contents to Benji when he visited again. She rehearsed the conversation all the time. She had begged Benji to continue to visit until she recovered completely. Benji promised to do so.

Another day, Benji went to the hospital to see Hattie. Hattie was not there. Benji panicked. What happened? he asked.

The doctor told him that Hattie was flown to US that morning for a specialized treatment.

"Heavens help!" Benji cried. "Did she get worse?"

"Not necessarily," replied Dr. Cohen, "we found that her injury was complicated, and decided to send her to the United Stated to receive an advanced treatment. If we were to work on her leg here, she might end up losing the limb. We don't have the equipment for the type of surgery she needed."

Benji was devastated. He would've loved to see Hattie before she left. He was heartbroken. He had brought her some presents among which were a ring and rose flower. Hattie would've loved to have the ring, no doubt. Distressed by the unexpected news, he kept the rose flower on her empty bed and went home wondering if he would ever see Hattie again. Oh, my Hattie, he moaned. I had wanted to tell her that I loved her so much; that she would be mine forever; that she was the most beautiful woman in the world; that she was my Queen and my golden pearl; that she should keep her love for me; that I'd do whatever it takes to have her forever; that my love for her was immeasurable; and that I want to marry her.

Unfortunately Hattie was gone and the possibility of seeing her again was remote. If Benji had off-loaded these pleasant thoughts to the girl the last time he was with her in the hospital, he would've been satisfied that Hattie had gone with his intention.

In this life, time waits for no man. If you have any good things to do or to say to a loved one—parent, brother, sister, friend, especially a spouse—make haste to do so while there is time. For you never know if you will have the opportunity to do so later.

CHAPTER 31

When Benji was fully recovered, he went back to his relief work with the Red Cross. Mr. Gardner was pleased to have him back. Benji was one of his best workers. Mr. Gardner had told him how devastated he was when the aftershock trapped him in the ground. He hired Benji and gave him a double promotion followed by an official admission into the International Red Cross Society. Benji was registered as a life member of the organization.

By March (2010), the activities of the relief workers in Haiti had slowed down. The emergency segment of the Red Cross began to shift attention to other areas of disaster in different parts of the world. Benji was detailed to Indonesia where there was a recent earthquake. He worked in Indonesia for one month and was sent to the

Red Cross Headquarters in the United States for training. After the training, he had two options—to work for the International Red Cross Organization full time, or to pursue his own career while remaining a member of the Red Cross, to be recalled for emergency services any time anywhere.

Benji decided to pursue a Masters degree in Business Administration. Right away, he enrolled at the Waterside State University, New Jersey. With this, he swung back into the rhythm of life as a student. He met many international students, some of them were from Nigeria.

The thought about the girl he saved in Haiti never left Benji's mind. One of his priorities was to locate Hattie. He knew she must be somewhere in the United States. His heart had fallen for this Caribbean girl. Is she still in the hospital? he wondered, or has she recovered? She probably has recovered, it's about six months now. Where will she be for Jesus sake?

Benji had called many hospitals in the US to ask about Hattie. So far there was no luck. The US is a big country with many states. It was a herculean task trying to fish out a single patient from thousands of hospitals around the country. But he did not give up. He continued to search, hoping that one day, he would find a hospital with a record of a patient flown to the hospital from Haiti during the earthquake.

Another side of the coin was that Hattie might have gone back to Haiti after her recovery. If this was the case, the chances of meeting her were grimmer. It would be difficult to locate her in Haiti if Benji would decide to pursue that option.

CHAPTER 32

Nkiru was pursuing her Masters program at John Hopkins University, United States. She left Nigeria in December 2009. In the school dormitory, she shared a two-bedroom apartment with a Haitian girl. They were very friendly and lived peacefully. Nkiru confessed that she had never met someone like the Haitian girl.

The two girls were down-to-earth home-raised—not given to the life style of the modern youth. For example, they didn't care so much about fashion. They did not change wardrobes frequently. Although Nkiru was the daughter of a rich man she maintained low lifestyle. Instead of spending a lot of money on herself, she used it to help poor students. Nkiru preferred to call her friend by her last name, Abiba. She said she liked her last name. Abiba called Nkiru "NK," which Nkiru preferred.

Nkiru treated Abiba like her younger sister. She was two years older than Abiba who was seventeen. Abiba was very respectful of Nkiru and submitted sequaciously to her instinctual motherly behaviours. She tidied Nkiru's room, laundered her clothes, and did many other things for her. Nkiru was very protective of Abiba and gave her all the support and guidance she needed to lead a successful college life. For example, Abiba, being a beautiful young woman, was a target for boys. Students often wanted to talk to her but not when Nkiru was around ready to clip them off. She spread her wings over Abiba against any approach she considered uncomfortable.

Abiba adhered to Nkiru's instructions and kept boys at a distance. She had resolved not to mess her life up. She devoted her life to one man only—the guy that rescued her from the Haiti earthquake. She did not know his name, but she thought she would recognize him if she saw him. She prayed that she would see him again.

CHAPTER 33

The memory of the Red Cross worker who saved her life at the Haiti earthquake, was still fresh in Abiba's mind. She found it extremely difficult to replace the image of this man with another. She remembered how he scooped her out of the heap of debris and he held her passionately in his arms in the rubble, cleaning and dusting her face. She recalled the affectionate kiss in the rubble, the warm hugs, the tender care, and the love this man gave her in the underground wreckage where she was trapped by the earthquake. Not even my mother had given me such a passionate care, Abiba said to herself while reflecting on her experience in the rubble.

Abiba often talked about this guy. She often told Nkiru about the circumstances under which she met him. She narrated her experience of the Haiti earthquake—how she spent days under the wreckage of a two-storied building. She also told Nkiru that she loved the guy so much and would be glad, not only to see him again, but to marry him.

"You guys met beneath the earthquake rubble?" Nkiru asked.

"Yes, I was half dead when he dug me out of the dust," Abiba related. "He was one of the rescue workers during the earthquake. He came to the piles of wreckage and met me buried in the heap of debris and brushed off the piles of filth that covered my body. He held me passionately and protectively from a devastating aftershock that almost killed both of us. When I regained consciousness in the hospital bed, they told me that nobody wanted to go into the underground where I was trapped to save my life for fear there might come another earthquake and walls would collapse upon them. There were several aftershocks that followed the earthquake. But this young man volunteered, crawl into the twenty-feet ditch, and save my life. Oh, Heavens! Please keep this man for me," Abiba prayed.

"Do you love this guy?"

"To death!"

"Did he promise to marry you?"

"He did. I know he loves me passionately. In fact, there was no time for us to talk in the rubble. We were chiefly concerned about getting out alive. After he had brushed my face, I asked him to kiss me before I die, for I thought I was going to die."

"Did he kiss you?"

"Oh, he did, a passionate kiss; an unforgettable kiss. And he was the only man that had ever kissed me."

"You shouldn't have let him go out of your life." Nkiru regretted.

"Our separation was impromptu," said Abiba mournfully. "Immediately we were rescued from the pit, I was rushed unconscious to the hospital. He visited me in the hospital, but two days after, I was flown to the United State for treatment. I never saw him again. I don't even know his name. I wish I could see him again to thank him for saving my life. I could've died if he had not volunteered to crawl into the tunnel."

"What a nice guy!" Nkiru exclaimed, watching Abiba sympathetically.

"NK, he was such a sweetheart."

"You may meet him again, you never know," said Nkiru.

"I wish so."

"Condition your mind to meeting him. It's possible that you guys can meet again. Sometimes what we wish for and pray for, comes true, whether it is evil or good. It may not come exactly as we wished."

"Oh mother Mary, send this man back to me," Abiba prayed again.

That night, Abiba did not sleep. She was thinking about the man who saved her life. I can't forget that passionate kiss, she thought. Will I ever see him again? Will he ever kiss me again? Oh, I wish I knew his name.

That kiss in the rubble was indeed Abiba's first kiss ever. Stuff like kissing was strictly forbidden in her house. Her parents tailored their children's upbringing to reflect the spiritual life of purity and sanctity. No boy friends, no girl friends, no movie, no club or partying, no bad company, no romantic literature, and so on, until they got married. All five of the children adhered devoutly to this principle. Abiba, for one, was guarded by this injunction until age 17 when a strange man kissed her underneath the earthquake wreckage. She yielded completely to the kiss. In fact, she asked for it, having developed attachment to the man who kept her company in rubble.

CHAPTER 34

At the campus, of John Hopkins University, Nkiru enquired from African students whether they knew a student from Nigeria whose name was Benji Anigbo. Nobody knew anyone by that name. She searched and searched, no luck. She wished she could find Benji. She thought he must be somewhere in US.

The United States of America is a large country with many States. There are hundreds and thousands of colleges and universities. It would be difficult to locate a student in more than fifty states. Nkiru did not give up. She kept trying, hoping that some day someone would give her some useful information.

"By God's grace, I must find him," Nkiru told Abiba one day while they were heading to their hostel after class.

"I hope so," Abiba sympathized solemnly. We will eventually find our respective lovers wherever they may be."

"We will," Nkiru said. "I love this boy so much."

"You do?"

"Yes. And the irony is that my father did not want me to marry him."

"Wh—y?" Abiba lamented subjectively.

"He had no reason, other than that Benji was from a poor family."

"That's ridiculous."

"I know. I did everything I could to convince my dad to the contrary, he would not budge. He insisted that I must marry a man of high calibre, someone from a wealthy and influential family like him."

"Are you from a royal family?"

"Yes, I am. My father is the younger brother of the King of my town."

"I see. But he should allow you to make your choice of a man." Abiba argued. "Is this boy ugly or something?"

"Oh no, Benji is cute! He is athletic, robust, and physical. He is handsome and very good mannered. I'm yet to see a man who could love a woman the way Benji does. Oh, my Ben!"

Abiba saw Nkiru's eyes crystallized with tears. She looked away to allow her to stifle the tears. "I can't understand why your dad would not allow you to marry the man you loved, in this civilized age."

"Actually, my father told me I could marry whoever I liked, but he must be from a prominent family."

"Well, that restriction is not appropriate. It's still equivalent to marrying his choice."

"I agree with you. *Put the goat in the tether, and put the tether on the goat, are they not the same thing?* I disagreed with my father over this issue. He is stringent and has an authoritarian personality. My people should be happy he isn't the King of the village. If he were the King, his leadership would've been unspeakably despotic, autocratic, and tyrannical. I fought tooth and nail to assert my rights over this issue but he told me he would destroy the person, disown, and banish me, if I go against his will."

"You're in trouble," said Abiba sympathetically. "What are you going to do since this is the man that won your heart?"

"Nothing short of marrying him. I will marry Benji, unless I cannot find him anywhere in the world."

They were still talking when one of the Professors hailed Nkiru from the parking lot. "Come here, please."

Nkiru looked at the man and pointed to herself.

"Yes, you," the professor said.

Nkiru handed Abiba her school bag and walked across the parking lot where the Professor was waiting. "Hi." She greeted him.

"How are you doing?" he asked.

"Doing good."

"I have seen both of you several times in the student traffic, and I guess you are both from Africa."

Nkiru wondered if the man was taking a census of students from Africa. "Oh yes, we're from Africa. Oh, correction, I'm from Africa. My friend is from the Caribbean."

"Oh, is that right? By the way, my name is Idris."

"I know your name Professor. My name is NK."

Mr. Idris laughed to hear that he was well known. "Did you say NK?"

"Yes, NK, short for Nkiru."

"Okay, nice to meet you NK."

"Nice to meet you too," Nkiru smiled.

"From your name, I deduce you are Igbo."

"Yes. And you are Yoruba?" Nkiru smiled again.

"Yes. Well NK, I want to tell you that I like your friend. What's her name?"

"Abiba."

"Abiba?" Professor Idris repeated. "I'm highly interested in her. As I said, I have often seen both of you pass by, and I said I must talk to you about what I'm thinking. But I prefer to do it the African way, that is, to speak with you first, then, you will convey my feelings to your friend. After that, I will have a chat with her, depending on her reaction. She is such a pretty image. I think about her every night. Do me a favour NK, tell Abiba that your brother is dying for her; that I would like her to be mine if she thinks that I can be her future partner."

"I will. I'll tell her what you said."

"How do you think she would react . . . ?"

"Hmmm, I don't know what her reaction would be, but I promise to speak with her about your thoughts."

"Good. I trust you. Do all you can to market me."

"I'll try."

CHAPTER 35

"What was he saying to you?" Abiba asked Nkiru.

"He is interested in you," Nkiru replied and laughed.

"Interested in me?" Abiba frowned her face.

"Yes. The professor says he likes you."

"Why?"

"Why? He likes you as a man would like a woman. What's wrong with that? He said he had often seen us walk by, and that he was interested in talking to you. He said you're pretty and that he wanted me to tell you that he would like to talk to you."

"Talk to me about what?" asked Abiba.

"I just told you. He wants to talk about a relationship."

Abiba blushed. She seemed not interested in any relationship, whether student or professor.

"Well, my study first. I don't care about . . ."

"Listen," Nkiru said, "on a serious note, you never know *where a precious pearl can be found.* You never know if this is the man God has sent for you."

"I don't . . ."

"This guy is handsome. And he is young. He probably completed his study in this school and they found him very intelligent and offered him a teaching position. You hardly find many young teachers in a renowned institution like John Hopkins."

"You're quite right. Good schools are very picky about their teachers and seldom employ young teachers except the bright ones."

"He is from Nigeria," Nkiru continued.

"Is he?" Abiba said and relaxed the tension on her face.

"Yes, he is from Nigeria."

"Nigerian students are very bright," said Abiba as she opened the door of their apartment. She threw her school bag on the sofa and sprawled on the carpet. "I knew one boy from Nigeria, his name was Professor Ofor-ka-si. He was teaching mathematics in my school back home in Haiti. And, did you remember that young man who gave us some coins at the soda machine last week?"

"The guy from Nigeria?" Nkiru asked.

"Yes. He is a professor at the Department of Microbiology. His name is Fred Achu . . . Achu-si-fu. Am I right?"

"Achufusi," Nkiru assisted her.

"Thank you, Fred Achu-fu-si. He is about twenty-five or twenty-six years. Your people have many young brains."

"Thank you," Nkiru acknowledged.

Abiba was thinking. She looked blank.

"Think about it," said Nkiru, parting her on the shoulder. Professor Idris is a very handsome man. He is young and smart. What else?"

"Hmmm," Abiba sighed. "And he is from Nigeria."

"There you go."

CHAPTER 36

Abiba pulled off her trousers and flung them into a chair. She did her top the same, leaving only her pant and bra. "Since I met that nice guy from Nigeria at the earthquake site in Haiti, I have come to admire people from that part of the world."

She sat down and spread out her long smooth legs.

Nkiru looked at her legs and teased her, "Professor Idris will like those legs."

They laughed.

Abiba had a nice pair of legs. She ignored Nkiru's comment about her legs. She had heard such comments several times, not only about her legs but also about her entire feature—her nice bodily shape, her romantic eyes, her dense eyebrows, her sexy long hair, her long neck, her dimples, and her flabby belly.

"Professor Idris has many good things to win your love," Nkiru said. Counting on her fingers. "First, he is a Nigerian, that's point number one; you said you like Nigerians. Point number two, he is smart. Three, he is young. Point four, he is teaching in a popular school. Point five, he is handsome. Point six . . ."

"Handsomeness for a guy is not a strong point," Abiba ruled, opening her McDonald lunch packet. She picked up a french-fry. "The qualities women look for in a man, in my opinion, are: loving, caring, achievement, strong physics, protection, trustworthiness, faithfulness, etc."

"Your list is good," Nkiru said trying to re-assemble her burger meal that was disintegrating. She was still learning to eat a hamburger in tact. "nonetheless, you cannot rule out handsomeness. If a man has all these good qualities but has a chimpanzee face, would you still go for him?"

They burst into laughter.

"Let me ask you something," said Nkiru sipping her soda. "You know that most immigrants, especially those from Africa, choose to go back to their country when they retire from service, assuming you marry a Nigerian man, would you be willing to go with him to Nigeria to spend the rest of your life?"

"Yes, of course," Abiba agreed. "I'll be more than happy to go with him. After all, that's where I came from."

"You are from Haiti."

"Yes, but originally I am from Africa. All the Blacks in South America, and in the United States, are from Mother Africa, remember?"

"Correct."

"The only problem is that no one knew where he or she came from in the African continent. These wicked people made every effort to obliterate the memory of the slaves, their background, their country of origin, the district, the town, the village, the clan or kindred, etc."

"That's too bad," Nkiru said regretfully as the conversation veered into a new dimension.

"Those of us who are the descendants of slaves regret that we do not know exactly where we came from in the continent of Africa. My father often said that if he knew to what part of Africa he belonged, he would've opted to return to that place and settle for the rest of his life."

"Oooh, that's very unfortunate." Nkiru said mournfully.

"One of the most painful experiences that Black Americans suffer today is the lack of knowledge of their exact extractions in Africa. The traces of their backgrounds in Africa were deliberately obliterated by the cruel slave owners. They will live with this pain forever."

"It's a pity." Nkiru lamented. "Man inhumanity to man."

"So if I marry a Nigerian, which I'm going to do any way, and he wants to move back home permanently, definitely, I'll be so happy to go with him."

"Abiba," Nkiru said, halfway through her meal, "I'm tired of fast food. Next Saturday we shall go to the African shop at Langley Park to buy African food."

"Yes, yes, yes! We shall go, and you will make *foofoo* and *ogbono* soup."

"I know you like *ogbono* soup and *garri*."

"Yes, I do."

CHAPTER 37

Benji was not relenting in his search for the girl he saved in the Haiti earthquake. He had combed almost one-fifth of the hospitals in the United States, none of them supplied information about a Haitian girl that was flown to US for treatment during the earthquake disaster in Haiti.

Not able to locate this girl, Benji turned his mind to Nkiru. Since he went to prison in Haiti for drug trafficking, he had never had any contact with his people in Nigeria. Now that he was settled in school in the US, he wanted to touch base with home folks, especially Nkiru. He tried to call Nigeria, but her number didn't go through. He thought Nkiru may have changed her phone number.

One day he saw a former schoolmate, Obinna, who was travelling to Nigeria. He asked Obinna to enquire about Nkiru,

"Do you know Enugu city?" Benji asked Obinna.

"I grew up in Enugu," replied Obinna. "I know all corners of the city."

"Good. Go to 220 Mbonu Street, Independence Layout, and check if a girl called Nkiru Aninwede is still living there. Also, find out if she is married or single. If she no longer resides in this address, find out where she has moved to."

"That's simple. I'll do that."

Three days after his arrival in Nigeria, Obinna went to 220 Mbonu Street, Independence Layout to fulfill his obligation to Benji. Some children were playing in front of the yard. "Hey come here," he called to one of them.

The boy turned but did not come. Their parents had warned them about strangers and kidnappers.

"These kids can be naughty," Obinna fumed. "Hey, I'm talking to you and you are playing. Pay attention!"

"Sorry," said another child among them. "How can I help you?"

"Do you know Nkiru Aninwede, she lives in this yard?"

"No, we just moved in here," replied the boy.

The other boys had converged around the stranger. One of them told Obinna that the girl he was looking for no longer lived in that house.

"Do you know where she lives now?"

"No, but her room-mate may know, she is still living here."

"Great. What's her name?"

"Chelcie."

"Okay, thank you guys."

Obinna moved briskly to the house. The children looked at him and laughed.

"He looks like someone from America," said one of the boys.

"How do you know?" another boy challenged.

"Because his trousers are dropping off his butt, and he speaks: *I wanna, I gonna, Hey me-en!*"

Obinna met Cheluchi who told him that Nkiru had gone to the US a year ago.

He was satisfied that he got some information for Benji.

He came back to the children, fumbled in his pocket, and gave them a twenty-dollar bill, "Take this for your biscuits."

"Thank you Sir, thank you Sir," the children chorused admiring the dollar note. They had never seen a foreign currency. They abandoned their play and ran inside to celebrate the windfall.

CHAPTER 38

Nkiru and Abiba exited from the Metro bus, crossed the street, and went into the African store to buy Nigerian foodstuff. They had been looking forward to it. Nigerian food is available in US, however, it's too expensive, besides, you don't have the time to cook. Nkiru and Abiba will cook today, it was a public holiday. They will enjoy a Nigerian home-made dish. Abiba, in particular, was dying for Nigerian food. She had become addicted to Nigerian dishes, infact, everything Nigeria.

Immediately after they stepped into the African store, Nkiru saw what looked like a familiar face. She wondered if this was Mabel. Mabel turned around and saw her and cried,

"My God! Nkiru!"

"Heeey! Mabel!" Nkiru shouted. They embraced each other, shouting and screaming. Abiba stayed aside, watching and smiling. Nkiru turned to her, Abiba, this is Mabel, she is my country girl and a very good friend back home.

"Hi Mabel," Abiba smiled, giving Mabel a slight hug.

"Mabel this is Abiba, my room-mate at John Hopkins."

"Hi Abiba," Mabel greeted.

"Mabel!" Nkiru said admiring the store lady. "How have you been?"

"I'm doing great."

"I can see it. You look good."

"Thank you, so do you. When did you come to the US?" Mabel asked Nkiru moving over to the counter to attend to a customer.

"About a year ago. I've been to this store a few times, I didn't know it was yours."

"Yes-oo, it's mine. My husband keeps the store. I come here occasionally to relieve him, especially when he has some place to go. That's how we are managing life. It's not easy to secure a job in this country, especially if you are a foreigner."

"My sister, tell me about it," a customer from Ghana chipped in. That's what I am battling with now." It's difficult to secure employment here, contrary to what we were told back in Africa."

146

"Exactly," Mabel agreed. "Back in Nigeria, people often speculate that America is littered with treasures and jobs, and that as soon as you touched down at the airport, different jobs are waiting for you to make your choice, no hassle."

"That was my thinking back home," the customer said. "I thought that I would get a job immediately after I arrived in America."

"Never!" said Mabel. "When my husband finished his studies, he couldn't get a job. Because he had to pay his bills, he worked as a security man for years, he worked at the McDonald restaurant, he worked as a pizza-delivery man, a cab driver, and a truck driver. The list is endless. All this while, he was hoping that one day he would obtain a better job, but none came. Despite this difficulty, folks at home call our house every day to ask for doll . . ."

"Oh, they have started calling me already asking for money," Nkiru said. "Just this morning a relative woke me up and began to ask why I have not started sending them dollar."

"They think that dollar litters all over the place in America," Mabel said handing some change to the customer who was checking out, "and that you only have to scoop as much as you can."

"I wish some of them could come here and see things for themselves," another customer from Africa said.

"Exactly." No matter how you try to explain the situation, they will not understand. They simply feel that you are there enjoying life and do not want to help your people who are suffering at home. They don't realize that people over here are really suffering. My husband will never forget the pains and distress he went through inorder to survive in this country. Yet his brothers accuse him of playing about with women and enjoying himself in US."

While the conversation was going on between Nkiru, Mabel, and the customer, Abiba was waiting. She had collected the food they needed and wanted Nkiru to vet the items before the checkout.

"Mabel, since I know that you are here," Nkiru said, "I will be coming occasionally for a chat."

"That will be wonderful. I'm so glad to see you today."

"Me too."

"Nkiru, before you go," Mabel said thoughtfully, "may I ask if you have seen Benji, I think he is in US?"

"No," Nkiru replied miserably, "I heard he is in US, but I've not seen him. I've been trying to find him. America is a vast country. Looking for a person here is like looking for a grain of sand in a sand-dune. Since you have been here for a while, if you happen to see anyone from Nigeria please ask if he or she knows Benji."

"I will," replied Mabel. "My husband knows many people from our place. I will talk to him."

"We shall talk later," Nkiru said and took Abiba by the hand as they headed to the door.

"Your friend is pretty," Mabel remarked, "I hope you find her one of our boys to take her home to Nigeria."

"That will definitely happen," Nkiru laughed and looked at Abiba who also smiled at the compliment.

CHAPTER 39

The whiff of the rich African meal Nkiru and Abiba were cooking had begun to waft across the dorm. Residents were sniffing at doors wondering who was cooking. They wanted to know, and perhaps visit the person. The powerful scent of *ogili (*an Igbo seasoning) was airborne throughout the hostel stirring hungry students. Nkiru and Abiba had locked their door firmly. They did not want any disturbance. African food is expensive in America. They didn't want to share.

Soon the food was ready. Abiba sat on the floor like the Muslims. "This type is not eaten at the dinning table," she said. "I'm staying on the carpet."

"Of course," Nkiru agreed. "You enjoy this better relaxing on the floor."

They ate their food in peace and chatted. Abiba spread her long legs full length attacking the ogbono soup and garri-foofoo. Nkiru looked at her legs again and said,

"You've got a nice pair of legs, Abiba."

"Thank you," Abiba replied, very busy with her meal.

"I must find you a Nigerian boy who will be happy to own those pretty limbs."

"That's what I want."

"And you will go with me to live in Nigeria."

"Yes. I want to go back to my root. It's nice to have a background. Those of us from South America and the United States wish that we had background where we can return at old age like you guys."

"Actually blacks have a background," said Nkiru munching goat meat, "but the issue is that they cannot trace their exact places in the continent of Africa. They do not know the countries, the cities, the towns, the villages, the clans, and kindred they came from."

"Exactly, that's our greatest agony."

"I heard that some Black Americans are now engaged in digging into archives through the DNA processing, to trace their origin in Africa."

"Don't listen to them," Abiba said flippantly. "Americans can make money by any means. The people who carry out these studies can falsify or create history in order to satisfy their clients who are anxious to get the information. My grandfather told me that the white people erased all traces of Black slaves. He said they did it on purpose."

"I think so," said Nkiru.

"If they wanted to keep information about the slaves at that time, they could, it wasn't impossible. The obliteration of records about slaves was deliberate. After all, there were several contemporary incidents and events that took place in those days around the Western World, and many of them were well recorded. Why couldn't they document information about the slaves?"

"I agree with you," said Nkiru. "They even suffocated their languages which would've been a sure avenue to determining who came from where. The Black brothers and sisters in this country are distraught that they have no place to go."

"We can go to any African country and settle," Abiba said. "These days, some Black Americans have resorted to migrating to any African country of their choice, buy a piece of land (land is very cheap in Africa), build a nice home, and naturalize in that area."

"Really?"

"Yes. My father told me that this is what many Blacks, who feel embittered, do. He said there are two inborn defects in the White man: hatred and pride. The Blacks are scapegoats."

"Ooooh. I feel for the Blacks," Nkiru moaned. "I was chatting with a student the other day on this topic and he brought up an ideology I did not like."

"What is it?" Abiba asked impatiently.

"He said that 'we' (i.e. their brothers and sisters in Africa), sold them to the white folks as slaves, and this was why they, and other Blacks in Diaspora were in this quandary situation."

"That's not a correct statement," Abiba snapped.

"It's not," Nkiru agreed and referred to the pedigree of her family, "My grandfather told me a different story about slavery. I'm from a royal family. My grandfather was a King. His father was a King, and his great grandfather was a King. Kingship was, and still is, in our ancestral dynasty. So our fathers, not only had first-hand information of the ontology of slavery, they were in direct contact with the White traders in different ways even before the *scramble for Africa* began.

"I would like to hear this," Abiba said and adjusted herself.

"Our Black brothers over here are taught the African history as written by the White man," Nkiru began. "My grandfather told me that during the occupation of African territories (divide and rule), by the White men, the colonialists who were running the governments of African nations, took native folks as house servants. These indigenous men and women voluntarily served the White settlers as house boys or house maids. When the white folks went to their land on vacation, sometimes they took their servants with them.

"The White relatives of the colonial masters overseas observed that the Black servants were very hardworking, loyal, dedicated, friendly, and what is more, they were physically very strong. Thereupon, the White folks overseas requested their colonial relatives in Africa to bring them Black servants from Africa to work for them as house keepers.

"According to my father, the demand for Black servants from overseas, and the supply from Africa, started here. The White folks at home, including those who owned plantations and farms, realized that the Black men who were sent to them from Africa were not only good farmers, utilitarian, and serviceable, but also highly industrious. They made more and more demands. The economic law of *demand and supply* kicked in.

"My father said that, initially, when African parents allowed their sons and daughters to serve the White man as cooks, gardeners, house-keepers, or messengers, it was free of charge. And it was voluntary; no force, no coercion, no malice. There were no payments. However, as time went by, the colonial masters began to compensate the servants and also to give their parents presents such as salt, mirror, machetes, gin and wine, etc., inorder to get more servants. In addition, they began to teach the servants their languages, ostensibly to be able to communicate with them to achieve their purpose. Knowledge of the White man's language facilitated communication between him and the natives, using the servants as interpreters too. As demand for servants became more pronounced, the White man gave out more presents, as inducement to recruit more servants. House help now received payments.

"One important thing to note here," Nkiru emphasized, "is that **parents gave the White men their children in the hope that those children would come back to them after a period of service. It was never the intension of the African parents to give away their children for sale.**

"My father said that as time went by, some White merchants, and business men in the Western world, who shipped merchandise to African countries, figured that they could make big money by recruiting more Black servants and workmen from Africa and sending them to big time farmers and plantation owners overseas.

"Thus, what we know today as slave trade began to develop between African countries and the Western world. My father also told me that some cruel and despotic Kings and Rulers in Africa, (like the greedy White merchants from the West), developed a great appetite for human trafficking. For example, instead of hanging criminals who committed felonies in the land, or killing tribal-war captives, some Kings and Chiefs handed these men over to the White folks to work for them. Weak children, especially those who played truancy in the farm, were also released to White colonialist to serve them. As the demand for workmen by the Whites escalated, some ambitious and greedy tyrants in Africa began to kidnap people to hand to the White traders (who saw more profit in human trafficking than rubber, cocoa, ground-nuts, hide, palm-oil, cotton, etc), in exchange for money. That was how it all started.

"Africans love and cherish their children. Their original intention was to please the White settlers by allowing their children to serve them as house help, and for their children to return home after the service. In their capitalist tendency, the White folks converted the generosity of the African ancestors into a business enterprise with human beings as the commodity. And, in an effort to absolve themselves from the crime of *man inhumanity to man,* they wrote the history upside-down, attempting to shovel the blames of slavery to the door-steps of the African ancestors."

"Oooh. Is that right?" Abiba cried. "This is a revelation."

"That's what my father told me," Nkiru concluded.

"Hmmmm!"

CHAPTER 40

Three weeks after their meeting at the African food store, Mabel called Nkiru and told her that there was some good news about Benji.

"Is that right?" Nkiru shouted excitedly.

"My husband searched the internet," said Mabel, "and came up with three Benjamin Anigbos. The web search did not give phone numbers on the listing, but there were mailing addresses of these people. If you have a pen, I'll give you the addresses.

"Oh, Mabel," Nkiru was breathless, "I'm so excited. Let me grab a pen.

Nkiru wrote three letters to the three Benjamins. She included her phone number, in case any of them would want to contact her. Three days later she got a phone call,

"Hello NK, NK."

"Who is this?" Nkiru replied.

"NK, this is Benji."

"Ooooooooooooh! Ooooooooooooh! Ooooooooooooh!" Nkiru yelled on top of her voice. "Benji, Benji."

"Yes, it's me."

"Ooooooooooooh! Ooooooooooooh! Is this Benji Chukwukadibia Anigbo?" Nkiru added Benji's middle name to be sure.

"Yes, that's me. How are you?"

"Is this my Benji?"

"Yes, it is. Girl, it's me."

"Ooooooooooooh! Good Lord! I can't believe you're the one. Ooooooooooh! Ooooooooooh! Ooooooooooh!" Nkiru kept shouting for joy. "My love Benjiiiiiiiii."

"That's me. How are you sweet-heart?"

"Benji, how are you doing? How have you been?"

"I'm doing great. What about you, love?"

"I've been looking for you," Nkiru said as she drew Abiba close to herself absentmindedly and coiled one arm around her neck joyously. Abiba was standing by, listening. She was equally excited for her friend. She couldn't wait to see this Benji that Nkiru loved so much.

"I've been looking for you too in US." Benji said pacing up and down his room.

"Who told you I was in US, love?" asked Nkiru.

"I asked a student, who travelled to Nigeria, to visit your house at Independence Layout Enugu. They told him that you had left the country for the United States."

"Oooooh! So you were looking for me, darling?"

"Of course, my love. Your address reads John Hopkins University; are you at John Hopkins?"

"Yes," Nkiru replied.

"That's a good school."

"Really?"

"Yes, it's one of the best schools in this country. What course are you studying?"

"Benji, forget about courses for now, we shall talk about school later. How is your health my love?

"I'm fine," Benji replied sizing himself in the mirror. He pulled proudly at the scanty whiskers growing on his jaw. "I'm doing pretty well."

"Are you sure?"

"Yes. Why?" he contorted his face.

"Because, in the message you sent me when I was in Nigeria, you were lamenting about suffering. You seemed to be in distress. I almost died of depression after receiving that message. I thought you were going to die. Are you sure you're okay?"

"Girl, I'm quite healthy. For now, leave the contents of that message, dear. It's a long story. I'll give you a detailed account of my journey to America."

Benji and Nkiru talked at length on the phone. Nkiru did not want to get off the phone. They covered many topics in their conversation but left many things untouched. Benji promised to visit Nkiru at John Hopkins. The girls could not wait to see him.

CHAPTER 41

While Nkiru and Benji were on the phone, Abiba was sitting nearby waiting. She already knew, from what Nkiru was saying, that this was the man she told her about. No sooner had Nkiru got off the phone than she asked hastily,

"NK, who's that?"

Nkiru began to dance joyful.

"Talk to me girl," Abiba repeated impatiently, "who was that person?"

"Of course you know already," Nkiru replied still dancing and smiling. "It's my boy, Benji."

"The one you have been searching for?"

"Yes. I have found him. Oh, glory be to God. I never knew I was going to see Benji again in my life. Thank you Jesus. Who says prayers do not work? Thank you Jesus, thank you my Lord."

"I can't wait to meet Benji," Abiba said enthusiastically. She was happy for Nkiru, and she expressed this candidly.

A day before Benji's visit, Nkiru and Abiba went to the African food store to purchase some food items for a small party they planned for Benji. Nkiru already knew the type of food Benji relished—*egusi soup* with goat meat and foofoo. They did not invite anybody. They wanted to celebrate the re-union among the three of them. Benji had told Nkiru during one of their phone conversations that he had not tasted Nigerian food since he left the country. Nkiru had assured him that he was going to enjoy it when he came to her house.

The next morning, the girls began to cook. Benji had a good appetite, Nkiru knew this. She prepared enough meal for everybody. She had bought two hind legs of goat-meat for a super dish. They promised themselves a scrumptious celebration.

Not long after the food was ready, there was a knock on the door. Both girls rushed to the door holding their breath.

"Heeeeeeeeey Benji!" Nkiru shouted and leapt unto the stout and handsome looking young man.

Benji dropped his briefcase, held Nkiru, and lifted her up in the air, "My sweet darling."

"Ooooooh, my love," said Nkiru gleefully kissing Benji all over his face.

"Thank you my dear," Benji replied laughing animatedly. "I'm glad to see you again."

Abiba was watching. She was assessing Benji. What a fabulous man, she thought. He is awesome, goodness me!

Nkiru turned to her, "Abiba, this is Benji whom I have been telling you about."

"Hi Benji," Abiba said, diffidently. She curved her lips in an enthusiastic smile.

"Benji, this is Abiba, my room mate and my best friend, in fact my sister."

"Hi Abiba," Benji greeted with a warm handshake and sweet smile.

Greetings over, they sat in the living room chatting.

"Benji," Nkiru said cheerfully scanning him all over, "you look heavier and robust than you were before."

"Oh yea?"

"Yes."

"But I weigh only 180 lbs."

"He looks good like this," Abiba remarked. "I wouldn't think he weighs too much. And he is handsome."

"Thank you," Benji acknowledged Abiba's compliment.

"Yes, the boy is handsome," Nkiru agreed.

"The man," Benji corrected her.

Abiba burst out laughing. Nkiru joined the laughter. Benji felt he shouldn't be called a 'boy' any more.

CHAPTER 42

Benji and his hostesses were knee deep in conversation. They talked for a long time, forgetting the nice meal waiting in the kitchen. And then, Abiba yawned and stretched her tall figure. Nkiru got the message—she was hungry.

"It's time to eat," Nkiru announced and headed to the kitchen. Abiba followed behind.

"Abiba, set the table," Nkiru told her.

"Okay," Abiba replied and went to organize the dinning. Nkiru always behaved like a mother towards Abiba. She loved Abiba so dearly, and vise versa. They were more than friends to each other. They behaved like siblings towards each other. They were inseparable like *salt and oil* or *beetles and dung.*

Throughout the course of their conversation, Benji was watching Abiba unobtrusively. Time and again their eyes met. Benji was wondering in his heart if he had met this girl somewhere. She looks a bit familiar, he said in his heart, and she is pretty. I have never seen such a pretty face, he thought. She looks like something sent down from heaven to show the humans what beauty is all about.

Again, while they were at table, Abiba's eyes met with Benji's every now and then. Looks like he is watching my table habit, Abiba alerted herself. I must be careful how I chew and swallow, and how I lick my fingers.

From the moment Benji arrived, Abiba was wondering if she had seen this face man, for he looked a bit familiar. I probably have seen this face before, she said to herself. I like his physique. He's such a fabulous creature with a great personality. He exudes energy and vitality. Nkiru is lucky to get this specimen of a man.

"The soup is delicious," Benji remarked, "and it's my favourite soup."

"Yes darling, I know you like *egwusi* soup," Nkiru said wiping a drop of soup on her shirt. "That's why we cooked it for you."

"Thank you sweetheart," Benji said rubbing a hand on his belly. "My stomach is bursting."

166

"Eat as much as you like love, Nkiru told him, "because you don't see this type every day in US."

"I know," said Benji, "I'm tired of hamburgers and french-fries."

The meal was over. Everybody was full. They dragged themselves to the parlour. Again they plunged into conversation. As usual, Nkiru and Abiba sprawled out on the floor. Benji was relaxing on the sofa.

"Benji, when are you finishing?" Nkiru asked.

"I have one more semester to go," Benji replied and crossed his hairy legs. He wore short-knickers that fitted very well, not the baggy shapeless shorts that basketball players wear, or the saggy oversize things that teenagers wear these days.

Abiba eyed his legs. He has hairy legs, she thought to herself. He might have a hairy chest too. I like men who have hairy chest. One can always rub a hand on it.

"And after graduation, what next?" Nkiru continued to ask. She probably wanted to know Benji's plan regarding their future. They had not touched anything personal about their wrecked relationship; about the incident that contributed to Benji's sudden departure to America; about Chelcie's ugly behaviour; and about other things in general.

"After my graduation," Benji replied complacently, I will take the next plane back to Nigeria."

"What? There's no job at home. You must have forgotten that we have a terrible unemployment in Nigeria."

"I don't need a job." Benji said unruffled."

"What do you mean?" Nkiru was puzzled.

"Whether government or private, I don't need a job. I'll establish my own business."

Nkiru looked at him and laughed cynically. "How are you going to do that? You don't have any capital, church rat."

They all burst out laughing. Abiba laughed most. She was amused by the demeaning comment Nkiru made, but she admired the confidence in Benji's comportment. He seems to be a man at peace with himself and in harmony with the world, Abiba thought as she studied Benji with keen interest.

"I'm not prepared to work for anybody," Benji repeated, "rather, people will work for me. I'll be calling the shots. I'll establish my own business."

"I have heard that," Nkiru said incredulously. "I know it's dignifying to be self-employed, but my point is: where is the money? You don't have capital. *You don't chase the palm-eater bare-handed, neither can you run a horse-race without a horse.*"

"Don't worry about money," Benji said impressively as he crossed and uncrossed his legs. He was in the habit of crossing and uncrossing his legs when he made a point.

CHAPTER 43

Benji had money. He had more than enough to establish a business, but he didn't want to disclose anything yet. Most men have a way of dealing with the contents of their hearts; most women don't. Some women do not have control over their intra-personal communications as well as the hidden matters in their heart chambers. Our fathers used to say that: *What a man sees and shakes his head, a woman sees and screams.*

When Benji and his friend, Lambert, were working for a drug cartel in Haiti, they were saving their money in the bank. They were well paid. The business of drug-running in the Amazon jungle in South America was dangerous but it is money-making. However, most drug runners never lived to enjoy their money. Benji survived.

During the operations at the Amazon rainforest, Benji always had his bank passbook in his pocket. Apart from his Holy Bible, the passbook, and a piece of paper where he chronicled events, he had nothing else in his possession. When he was being taken to his cell, he had the bank-book tucked inside his Bible. During the check-in, he asked the officials if he could take his Holy Bible with him.

"Sure," the Warder replied, "You are going in for a long term, so you can take as many Bibles as you like, if that will serve you any purpose, fool."

Benji thanked his God and went into the cell with his treasure. He continued to protect it until the day the Haiti earthquake destroyed the penal complex allowing inmates to escape.

Benji had over half a million dollars saved in his bank account. With this kind of money, he could start any medium-size business in Nigeria. This was where his hope lay. He planned a lot, but revealed very little.

The following morning, they assembled at the dining table for breakfast. Benji had taken his bath and appeared in a sparkling T-shirt with a Red Cross symbol. Nkiru was slicing the bread. On the menu were fried eggs, canned-beef, orange juice, peak milk, sugar cubes, and ovaltine beverage. The African grocery stores in US have almost everything Nigerians eat.

Today Nkiru sliced the breakfast bread. Abiba knew why—they had a visitor. Normally they would rip small pieces at a time, dip it in the tea, and eat. Abiba liked to eat bread and tea the African way. That was how her parents ate bread and tea at Haiti, and that's how she and Nkiru ate their bread-breakfast. But today, they had a visitor and had to eat bread via the sandwich.

"I like your T-shirt Ben," Abiba said with a candid smile.

"Thank you," Benji acknowledged, adjusting his sandwich.

"Yea, I have been looking at that polo shirt," Nkiru said. "Where did you get it?"

"Oh, I'm a member of the Red Cross Organization," Benji replied.

"Really?"

"Yea?"

"How come, did you join them at school?" Nkiru asked and sipped her beverage.

"No. I joined the organization in Haiti."

Immediately Benji mentioned Haiti, Abiba stared at him wide-eyed.

"Abiba is from Haiti," Nkiru noted.

"Yes, I'm from Haiti." Abiba nodded smiling.

"Oh yea?"

Nkiru was a bit confused. She never heard that Benji went to Haiti after leaving Nigeria. "How come, when, how did you get to that place?" she asked. "What were you doing in Haiti?"

"It's a long story baby," Benji sighed and smiled.

Benji had not revealed his expedition yet. He and Nkiru had not discussed any details about his adventure in Haiti. They would've done so last night when they went to bed, but Nkiru would not sleep with him. That would've been a better time to talk about private matters.

Benji had asked to sleep with her, she declined. She explained that she did not want to create a situation that might hurt her friend's feelings.

"If we isolate her," Nkiru told Benji solemnly, "what do you think will be in her mind? *They have gone to do it.*"

"So what?" Benji argued. "Baby, are we not . . . ?"

"Stop there!" Nkiru interrupted him. "Go and sleep in my room. I'll sleep with Abiba in her room. We have plenty of time for everything."

"What are you talking about love?" Benji said lowering his voice.

"I know what I'm talking about, I'm a woman. I don't want to create any division yet. I don't want to make her feel bad."

"I can see you love this girl so much," Benji whined.

172

"More than I love my sisters," Nkiru replied adjusting the sleeve of her sparkling nightgown. "I'm very fond of her. She's my pet."

Nkiru looked magnificent in her nightgown. Tonight, she looked like an Angel on an errand. Her face was radiating glory. Her breast nipples were irresistibly erect, and seemed to point at Benji. Benji was mesmerized. He drew closer to grab them, but Nkiru pushed him away gently, "Go to my room."

"Honey, after all these years," Benji pleaded in his best masculine temperament.

"Go to my room," Nkiru chuckled, looking ravishing.

Nkiru had a strong moral disposition. Her chastity was exemplary.

Benji was disappointed, but he was understanding. He knew Nkiru very well. Within her personality structure, were buried a sweet disposition that was well known to him. He was the type that could handcuff his sexual desire.

Benji did not want to reveal his whole story here at the dining. Instead, he cut the account short:

"I was in that Caribbean country during the last year earthquake in Haiti. I joined the Red Cross to help the victims of the geological disaster. I worked with one Mr. Gardner who gave me some Red Cross shirts. I still have some in my house."

"I would like to have one," Nkiru requested.

"Me too," Abiba said shyly. "Do you know Mr. Gardner?"

"Yes, I worked with him," Benji replied. "Do you know him?"

"Yes, he and his rescue team worked at the L'Enfant District earthquake sectors where I was trapped underneath the collapsed building, about twenty feet deep. There was this young man who managed to crawl into the wreckage to scoop me up."

Benji sprang to his feet, looking shocked. He stared at Abiba, his eyes wide open and his heart pulsating.

"What is your full name?" he asked Abiba hastily, almost shouting.

"Hattie Ella Abiba," she replied.

"Jesus the Saviour!" Benji screamed and jumped across the table where Abiba was sitting and roped her up in a thrilling hug. "I'm that person. I'm the man who came to rescue you in the wreckage.

"Oooooooooooh! Oooooooooooh!" Abiba yelled on top of her voice on realizing that this was the very young man who was in the rubble with her. "Oooooooooooh! Oooooooooooh! Oooooooooooh—my Go-o-o-o-d!"

She clinched Benji tight in a passionate hug, tears pouring from her eyes. Everybody was stunned at the strange turn of events. They were speechless at the discovery. They kept staring at each other in a profound astonishment. Nkiru was watching the unfolding event.

She was amazed at the incredible discovery. Unbelievable! She thought.

"Hattie, Hattie," Benji shouted again and again wondering if this was real or a dream. "Incredible!"

At this juncture, the picture of the young girl he rescued in the earthquake ruins came alive in his memory. Hattie had changed a lot, so Benji could not recognize her. When he saw Abiba yesterday, he was wondering if he had seen this face before. But he could not remember. Equally, Benji had changed so much. He was heavier now. At Haiti, inside the ruble, Abiba did not see Benji's face because it was dark. In the hospital when he visited her, he wore sunglasses. So she did not really come to know him that well. Right now, the pictures of their features at Haiti began to resonate in their minds. They now recognized each other.

Suddenly Benji sprang to his feet, rushed into the room, grabbed his suitcase, and began to rummage through it. He came up with a photograph and a newspaper cutting. In the picture, was Benji carrying Hattie in his arms. The newsmen had taken this photograph when Benji was emerging from the collapsed building with Hattie in his arms. The newspaper cutting had a story commenting on the rescue operation and calling Benji a hero.

Benji showed the photograph to the girls. They were amazed beyond words. All this while, Hattie was wiping tears of joy.

"What a strange turn of events," Nkiru remarked as she studied the pictures. "This is indisputably your face Benji, and this is Abiba. Her limbs were dangling."

"Yes, she was unconscious when I brought her out of the tunnel. I thought she had died. Show us the leg that was pinned under a fallen wall," Benji told Abiba.

Abiba raised her right leg on the table. The scars of the wound were there but barely noticeable.

"There was no damage at all to the leg," Benji said rubbing a finger on the faint lines of stitches. "When I pulled the leg out of the slab, I thought the doctors would amputate it because it was badly shattered."

"The doctors at Howard University Hospital said I would've lost my leg if they had tried to work on it in Haiti." Abiba said.

"I know, that's why they flew you to US," said Benji. "I came to the hospital the following day to see you, Dr. Hekortzi and nurse Henrietta Baptist told me that they had flown you to US to receive specialist treatment. I was devastated."

"I felt the same way when they were taking me away. I was thinking of you."

CHAPTER 44

Back in his school at New Jersey where he was pursuing the Masters degree in Business Administration, Benji recounted what took place at John Hopkins. He was glad he had reconnected with Nkiru. He was also pleased to have found Abiba who he had been searching for. He was delighted at the miraculous turn of event. But wait, Benji was a confused man. Because of the way things unveiled, he was obviously in a quagmire. Who would it be among the two?

He was gazing at the wall in his house, thinking about this issue. Lines of deep concern furrowed his brow. He was beleaguered by the choice of two women. Who will it be? he asked himself. I feel like a fly caught in a spider's web.

After the discovery at John Hopkins University, Benji and Nkiru had settled their differences, and renewed their engagement vow. Nkiru had given Benji an account of what happened after he left Nigeria. Benji had narrated the misfortune he went through in Haiti.

Nkiru had told Benji that she later discovered he was innocent of the incident that took place between him and Cheluchi.

"Cheluchi confessed," Nkiru said.

"She did?"

"Yes. She told me she lied. The bitch caused the circumstances that gave birth to your sufferings and woes. You shouldn't have left Nigeria in such a state of the mind."

During their conversation, Nkiru apologized to Benji in tears for believing what Cheluchi had told her at first, and for refusing to hear his side of the story. She had knelt down and said,

"I'm sorry. I was completely devastated when that animal made the confession. I felt like seizing her by the throat and choking the whore to death. I cried every day for weeks. I never knew you didn't do it. Benji, you are a great man. You are a rare human specie. I kept asking myself if you will ever ever forgive me, and whether I still have a place in your heart for disowning you and for vowing never to have anything to do with you in this world."

"That's no big deal," Benji told Nkiru smiling calmly. "I had even forgotten the incident. I suspected that Cheluchi might have lied to you about the incident. I do not blame you, everybody would react the way you did. I knew that one day the truth would come to light."

Nkiru had also told Benji about her father's death. Armed robbers had kidnapped Chief Igboanugo Aninwede and demanded millions of Naira which the man refused to give them. They shot him and took the money any way. Benji was sorry to hear that.

CHAPTER 45

Benji had found Nkiru, the girl he loved with all his heart and the girl he promised to marry. He had also found Hattie, the girl he rescued from the earthquake disaster, and the girl he reaffirmed his pledge, at the hospital bed, to be with all his life. These facts flew in the face of the confused young man. It was a dicey inscrutable situation.

Ever since Abiba got out of the Howard hospital, she had been searching for Benji. She asked every Haitian and every Nigerian she met if they knew a Nigerian who worked with the Red Cross at the Haiti earthquake mishap. She was praying, and hoping to find Benji so that both of

180

them would get married. She couldn't stifle the thought of this man. Now she had found him. What next?

To say that Benji was caught in a cobweb over this matter was an understatement. It wasn't his plan to marry two women. He loved the ladies, and, in their respective circumstances, had promised each of them marriage. Now, who would he go with? He was confused.

At John Hopkins, after celebrating Benji's discovery, Abiba was having the roughest time of her life. On one hand, she was genuinely delighted that she had found Benji. On the other hand, she was completely devastated to discover that the man she was looking for, and building her future on, was the same man her friend, Nkiru, was looking for and building her future on. What a mess! What a twist of fate!

Since the beginning of the unfolding imbroglio, life had slipped into an uneasy rhythm for Abiba. She was depressed. Everything turned dreary. These days, she approached things without emotion. She was heartbroken. She lost her appetite and consequently began to lose weight. She became reclusive and no longer enjoyed most of the things she used to enjoy. She didn't apply make-up any more; she didn't make selections in her wardrobe; she simply reached for any dress. As a result, she looked disheveled.

Although she was still the pretty sweet girl she used to be, her appearance and mood had changed since she discovered that the man she hoped to be marry was the very man her best friend had engaged years back. Her expectations were blighted. She relapsed in a sulking mood, cried everyday, and brooded always with a swollen face. The happy discovery had turned sour and disrupted the equilibrium of her life.

Nkiru was not unaware of what was going on with her friend. She had no problem intuiting at Abiba's ailment. "Don't worry baby," she consoled Abiba during one of their long conversations over this matter. "It will be alright. I can understand your situation. There's nothing under the sun that has no solution, except death.

Abiba looked at her friend with earnest eyes. She forced a wan smile looking listless. She wiped her eyes.

"This is an inexplicable phenomenon," Nkiru went on to massage her friend's battered spirit. "This is a hash coincidence and a nasty twist of fate. It's unfortunate that it turned out that both of us were waiting, hoping, dreaming, and looking for the same man. But we will find a solution to it. Stop grieving. Come back to your usual self. You are loosing weight. I don't want you to lose your plump shape. Stop sorrowing, my baby. Be cool, life must continue. You are my best friend. One thing you can be sure of is: I won't let you down. I won't allow you to suffer. I can sacrifice anything for you. I love you more than you can understand. Nothing will change my love for you. Wipe your tears, I hate to see you like this."

"The anchor of my happiness has gone," Abiba said amidst sob. "There's no hope for tomorrow."

"There is hope," Nkiru reassured her, "I'm in charge"

After that consoling discussion, Abiba wiped her eyes.

Both ladies had a lengthy conversation on this matter. Nkiru's statements kept re-occurring in her mind each time she was alone. What does she mean by: *I am in charge, we shall find a solution; I can sacrifice anything for you*? Abiba asked herself. What solution? What sacrifice? Is she going to abdicate her man to me? If that is what she meant, I wouldn't like her to do so. She came into Benji's life before me. She was the first person to occupy this man's heart. Although Ben loves me and promised to be mine forever, things have changed. The pendulum has swung to Nkiru's favour. I know he wouldn't buy the idea of taking me and letting Nkiru go. They can get married. But I love Benji so much. I love him to death. He stole my soul in the rubble. He occupied my heart that very day he kissed me in the earthquake rubble. With that kiss, he took my heart with him. It's better if I had not known him. I will miss him. I will miss Nkiru too. I'll miss both of them. I will die. I can't stand their exit from my life.

My whole world is tied to these two people individually and collectively. They are the only family I have in the world today. My parents and my siblings perished in the earthquake disaster, what am I living for? Death, where are you? What are you waiting for?

CHAPTER 46

During his fourth visit at John Hopkins in December 2011, Benji and Nkiru had a far-reaching discussion about their future. Their graduation was approaching. Each of them had one semester to go, all things being equal.

"When you graduate," Nkiru asked Benji, "what are you going to do?"

"You've asked me this question before," Benji smiled.

"I know."

Benji looked at Nkiru with a genuine affection. He pulled gently at his growing little whiskers with guarded pride and replied: "I will take the next plane home to start my business. What about you?"

"Before I found you," Nkiru replied with a vacant look, "I had planned to work for some time in the United States. But now that things have changed, we can all go together after our graduation."

"When you say all, how many of us?" Benji inquired hesitantly.

"All of us," Nkiru repeated. "Everybody here."

"Including Hattie?"

"Yes darling."

"Is that what she wants to do?"

"She swore she will never part with me, and I feel the same way too. She has no family. Before we found you, she told me that the man who promised to marry her was a Nigerian, and that if she found him, she would go to Nigeria with him to live. As things turned out now, the man she was talking about; the man she was looking for, was you. She is devastated. She cries everyday."

"Poor girl," Benji said sincerely. "If that is the case, we can take her with us honey. I have no doubt that she can find a nice man in Nigeria to marry her, don't you think so? She is pretty. You can help her do the marketing and find a nice guy."

"You will do the marketing." Nkiru said laughing. "You did business administration. I doubt if she would like to marry another man."

"Meaning what?"

"She said she had built all her life around you."

"Well, it's a pity. I love her so much and would've married her if I didn't find you or if you had married another man. She's such a sweet thing."

"Nigerians marry two wives." Nkiru said cautiously.

"Jesus come! Where are you going with this?"

"Well . . ."

"That's unorthodox," Benji said, his face twisting. "Sweetie, you are talking like someone who is not in her proper elements. We are not Muslims, we are Christians."

"Some Christians marry two wives."

"In the olden days, that is. It's an old Igbo culture. And I have never heard that it's the place of a wife to recommend another wife to her husband."

"I see, but our men marry two wives, don't they?" she said defensively.

Benji scratched his head, a little irritated, "Darling, where are you going with all this? Are you dreaming?"

"Don't be pessimistic about this issue, sweetheart. Marrying two wives is not a crime, is it?"

"It's not, but it's illegal here."

"I'm not talking about *here*, I'm talking about home, Nigeria. Even here in America, some people marry two wives, or more."

"Who said so?"

"I have seen some of them," Nkiru argued. "My classmate has three kids; her husband has two children with another woman whom he visits regularly. Another classmate told us that he had one official wife and one unofficial wife, both with kids. The man said that if his official wife began to nag and yell more than his energy could contain, he would move over to the unofficial wife. And if the unofficial wife begins to wear him down, he would move back to the official wife and mend fences. That's how he shuttles back and forth, and life goes on. What do you call that, monogamy?"

"Hmmmm!" Benji sighed.

"Like bird-droppings, American men drop children here and there with women. For instance, in some families, a sibling group of five kids may all have different fathers and one mother. Who is deceiving who? Now if you analyze these two cultures comparatively, which one carries some value? Which is more responsible and secure for the children: to marry two wives and live as one family with both women and children under one roof; or to have many men fathering children with a single woman? In some cases the fathers of the kids are unknown. Do you know the statistics of single families and the divorce rate in this country? Do you know the number of children in this country without fathers?"

"Well, there are a lot of twists and turns in the American social life. The family system is in disarray. I have seen such things myself. They say you must not marry another woman unless you divorced the first one, but people keep women and concubines in this society more than King Solomon. Even some public figures indulge in this mess."

"They are only deceiving women, that's my interpretation of it," Nkiru said.

CHAPTER 47

Another day, Nkiru brought up this subject. "Darling, you did not give me a definitive answer about my question last time."

"Wait a minute," Benji frowned his face, "NK are you serious about what you are proposing, I thought we were just kidding ourselves?"

"This is a serious problem Benji," Nkiru said solemnly. "You have to sit down and think about it. This young lady has been looking for you, hoping to find and marry you. Under the rubble, of all places, both of you made a vow to have each other. She told me everything. Even before we found you, she told me she would die if she did not marry this man. I asked her what she would do if she could not find the man anywhere. She said she would die. I noted that this girl had built her life, her future, her entire world around you. She swore to me during our conversation that if she found the man and he refused to marry her, she would take her life. Don't joke with this, sweetheart."

"*You are in the driver's seat,*" Benji said scratching his head, "*and you are on the cliff, if the car plunges into the ditch, don't blame anybody.* Got it?"

"Got it. Are you referring to Abraham, Hager, and Sarah of the Bible legend?"

"I'm being dragged by the collar into an uncharted path," Benji mumbled.

"Be considerate," Nkiru pleaded. She had the heart of an Angel. "This is a girl who lost all she had in the world; her parents, her brothers and sisters; all died in their house during the earthquake. You were the only person she clanged to in the rubble. She might have survived because of you. Think again sweetheart, this girl is an orphan and she needs help. She needs a family."

Nkiru's eyes were illumined with tears, as she spoke. She was right. Abiba had become a complete wreck since she discovered that her whole family perished in the earthquake. Her existence became meaningless to her. Life was useless. Her attachment to Nkiru turned out to be a stress-controlling mechanism, without which she would've died of depression.

"Okay, now that she has found me and discovered that I was engaged to you even before I left Nigeria, where do we go from here? I'm not denying that she . . ."

"Why didn't you tell her at Haiti that you were already engaged?" Nkiru charged, a bit irritated. "Why did you solidify her hopes? Based on the promises you made to her, both in the rubble and at the hospital bedside, she had established her future in you. There is compelling evidence that you promised to marry her."

"Honey, circumstances can change a man's word and life. I told you all I went through in Haiti. Remember that I told you in my message (when I was in prison) to forget me and to find someone else, didn't I? I never knew I was going to see you again. I assumed you had moved on with your life. But later, I found you. Besides, people can make promises and not keep them; they can engage partners and disengage. What's all the fuss about promise?"

"Let's look at this matter from a different perspective, Abiba wants to stay with me, and I'll not refuse. I want her to go with us to Nigeria. She will find a man there."

"Exactly!" said Benji. "Now we are talking. And she is pretty, honey. She will find somebody she likes back home."

"Suppose she did not?" Abiba said coldly.

"Time will tell."

CHAPTER 48

Six months later, Benji, Nkiru, and Abiba, had graduated and were ready to return to Nigeria. Benji had bagged a Masters degree in Business Administration; Nkiru had a Masters Degree in Law; and Abiba secured the first degree in Broadcasting.

Before they travelled to Nigeria, they went to Haiti at Benji's request. Three objectives were to be accomplished in Haiti: First, Benji wanted to withdraw his money from the Manor Bank in Haiti. Second, he wanted to show the girls some of the earthquake disaster areas, especially the site where Hattie was rescued. Nkiru had insisted she wanted to see this place. Third, they planned to visit Abiba's uncle and his family.

They arrived in Haiti late in the evening and spent the night at Topland Hotel in Port-au-Prince, ready to go out in the morning for sight-seeing. Everybody was excited.

"Abiba, your country looks nice, Nkiru remarked with some reservation as they drove around the capital city the following day.

"Do you think so?" Abiba said and laughed suspiciously. "I'm not sure it's that nice. Haiti is one of the poorest countries in the Western Hemisphere. Remember, this is the capital city. I'm not sure there is another city in Haiti that is better than this."

Benji and Nkiru agreed with Abiba in her innocent assessment of her country. From what they had seen so far, Port-au-Prince, the capital city, was not better than Ado-Ekiti Local Government Area in Nigeria, or Enugu Local Government.

After seeing many places of destruction, they headed to the very site where Benji rescued Abiba. The building was Abiba's house where her parents and her four siblings were buried alive during the earthquake. Her aunt, who was visiting from the village, also died with them. Out of a family of eight, only Abiba came out alive.

On seeing the house where they lived and where her entire family was killed, Abiba became emotional. She was in tears again. Nkiru gave her all the comfort she could muster.

Benji took Nkiru around the wreckage. "I went in through this hole," he told her pointing at a small opening in the wreckage. The hole looked like a rodents' course.

"How could you have passed through this tiny opening?" Nkiru wondered.

"I just managed to squeeze in. I wasn't heavy then."

"I know. You used to be on the lean side. Hamburger and chicken wings have bloated you."

"He won't see hamburger any more," Abiba said as they walked around.

CHAPTER 49

After visiting the earthquake sites, they drove to Tilori village to see Abiba's uncle, Rev. Edward Marvin. Rev. Marvin and his family were delighted to see Abiba. They had heard that Abiba was flown to the United States of America following her injury at the earthquake. They also heard that she had recovered and had started school in US. They had not seen her since then.

On seeing her cousins Abiba began to cry again.

"You don't have to do that," Rev. Marvin consoled her. "Stop crying my child, we are here for you. Any time you come back home, we are here to receive you. Your cousins are here to stay with you. Although you lost your parents and siblings, we are always here for you. If you have any problem, let me know, and I'll do my best. I can never allow you to suffer. The tragedy that took away your entire family was a heartbreaking one. But there's nothing we can do to reverse it, than to pray to the Almighty God to give us the heart to bear the burden. Life is treacherous and hopeless."

After visiting Rev. Marvin and his family, the party flew home to Nigeria.

OTHER BOOKS WRITTEN BY THIS AUTHOR INCLUDE:

The Moonlight Tales,
The Apprentice Boy Part One,
The Apprentice Boy Part Two,
Please Don't Tell Her I'm in Jail.